ALPHA SQUAD

Friends and Foes

LORELEI MOONE

eXplicitTales

Copyright © 2017 Lorelei Moone,
Cover art by Silver Heart Publishing
Published by eXplicitTales
All rights reserved.
ISBN-13: 9781913930240

CONTENTS

———◆———

Friends & Foes   1

About the Author   161

CHAPTER ONE

Adam King could hardly contain his excitement during the five hour drive to Sevenoaks. This was their first assignment. The first time Alpha Squad had been sent off-base on official business. Even the cramped conditions in the back of the squad Land Rover weren't enough to dampen his spirits.

They'd made it. After seemingly endless weeks of training and numerous tests and challenges, followed by a month-and-a-half of waiting around for their first deployment, they were a real task force. This was their chance to prove themselves.

And with that, it was also the first time Adam felt he had become part of something bigger than just himself. He was part of a team which could really change the world. As such, he would do everything in his power to ensure he and his team mates did not fail this first real-world challenge.

"What are you smiling about?" Eric—Adam's older brother and superior on the squad—asked.

Adam scanned the inside of the vehicle. Three pairs of eyes were fixed on him.

Along with Eric, there was Cooper—the human Border Force agent who had struggled the most throughout Alpha Squad's training—and Blackwood, a slightly naive but nice enough werewolf from the Rannoch clan up in Scotland.

Meanwhile, Bentley—the oldest and by far the grumpiest human of the group—was doing his best to ignore the goings-on inside the Land Rover. He was probably still raw about being passed over for second-in-command. His previous experience in the Special Forces had instilled within him a sense of superiority and entitlement, which made it difficult for Adam to sympathize with him.

The remaining two team members and only females on the squad were their leader, Major Janine Williams, and her petite and somewhat shy assistant, Private Callahan. They sat in the front cab of the vehicle, out of view.

Adam shrugged.

"It's good to finally be off-base, isn't it?" he asked. Of course, that was only a small part of why he felt so cheerful, but he'd never been one to share his thoughts and emotions. Least of all with his older brother.

"It's been a long time coming," Eric agreed and sat back, folding his hands.

"What do you think we're meant to be doing in Kent?" Cooper, the only human other than Bentley asked.

"Help out with the refugees, I dunno," Adam said. "I'm sure you know everything already, don't you, bro?"

Eric closed his eyes. "We'll all be briefed by local police when we get there. But I can tell you that yes, it does kind of relate to the refugee camp."

Adam shrugged again. Eric had always been the more serious one. It did not come as much of a surprise that he was unwilling to share what he knew.

"I've never been to Kent," Blackwood, the wolf, said. "What's it like?"

Adam stared at him for a moment. He was an odd guy, that wolf. From their previous interactions, Adam had already found out that Blackwood had grown up in a very different place than the rest of them. Wolves famously kept to themselves. And Blackwood's pack, which made its home somewhere in some remote Scottish forest, was no different.

"I dunno, it's like any other place in England. Lots of greenery," Cooper spoke up. "The seaside's nice."

Adam leaned forward, attempting to catch some of the views outside the window. There was precious little greenery to be found. Perhaps things would improve once they got off the motorway.

———•———

Once they finally left the motorway and entered the town, the scenery improved only slightly before deteriorating yet again. As their vehicle headed straight for the local police station, an unwanted welcome committee had already arrived, clogging up part of the road. Considering the size of the modest town, a largish crowd had gathered outside the station, carrying banners and shouting slogans.

'Send them back!'

'Protect our children!'

'Sevenoaks for humans, not animals!'

These were just some of the messages these supposedly concerned citizens were trying to spread. Adam inhaled sharply and kept his eyes fixed on the ground as he and the rest of the team disembarked. Although he had grown up in the city, his base instincts still did not appreciate crowds, especially not angry mobs. It was obvious that whatever they'd been called in for had the local populace sufficiently riled up that matters could escalate at any moment.

The team, led by Major Williams and Eric, carved a path through the protesters, marching straight for the front door where two skittish looking policemen waited.

"Alpha Squad. Here to see your chief." Major Williams flashed her ID.

The policemen exchanged a sheepish look.

"What's Alpha Squad?" one of them said after a short pause. His question was hardly audible over the chanting mob behind them.

Adam glanced over at the major, who had adopted an imposing stance with her legs planted squarely and shoulders pulled back. Although he could not see her expression, she would undoubtedly be annoyed already. Although limited, any interaction he'd had with her throughout boot camp clearly demonstrated that she did not appreciate having her authority questioned, least of all by two lowly local policemen.

"We are here on official business and your chief is expecting us," she snapped. "Step aside or I'll have your jobs."

Another confused look and short pause later, and finally the two men gave in and opened the doors for Major Williams and the rest of the squad.

Even after the team entered the building and the doors closed behind them, the chants from the angry crowd outside could still be heard. As uncomfortable as Adam had felt outside, it was worse now. They were in unknown territory and surrounded by enemies. And although they had trained for a lot of things during boot camp, this was something else entirely.

"Major Williams, Alpha Squad," the major introduced herself at the reception desk while the rest of the team, including Adam, stood by sheepishly.

The man in his early twenties who sat behind the counter blinked a few times, then looked around, as though someone would magically show up to tell him what to do. When no help was forthcoming, he picked up the phone from his desk and turned around, cupping the receiver in his hand, possibly to muffle the sound. That made no difference to Adam's super-human hearing, of course.

"Yes, I have some people here. Alpha Squad. Yes, Sir. No problem, Sir."

The young policeman looked even more flustered when he finally turned around again.

"I do apologize. Please go inside."

Major Williams didn't hesitate. She went straight for the doors toward the left of the reception desk and led the whole team into the heart of the police station. The spacious room was abuzz with activity. There were uniformed policemen as well as those in civilian clothes. On top of that, there were also a fair number of people who seemed to be either suspects or witnesses.

It was especially the latter group of bystanders who eyed Alpha Squad apprehensively, almost fearfully. Adam looked down at himself and suddenly felt conscious of his own uniform. All black commando gear, combined with his already imposing stature… All of it was a bit over the top. The shock he could see in people's eyes told him as much.

"Major Williams," a rotund middle aged man said, approaching the team, his hand held out in greeting. "Chief Inspector Huddersfield."

The major accepted the gesture and nodded. "My team is at your service and ready to get to work straight away."

"All in good time. Why don't you make yourselves at home first? Have a cup of tea after your long drive down from…"

Major Williams didn't answer directly. Perhaps she intended for the location of their base to remain a secret. "I can assure you we are well rested. If we can get the briefing underway, and get ourselves set up in a suitable workspace, we'll be out of your hair in no time."

Adam instinctively glanced at the Chief Inspector's receding hairline as the major finished speaking. An unfortunate turn of phrase.

"Very well," the man conceded. "I'll have my lead detective on the case hold the briefing."

The major nodded, and the whole team watched as Chief Inspector Huddersfield marched off and disappeared in one of the offices leading off from the room they found themselves in.

The conversation had been civil and polite, at least on the outside, but Adam had picked up on an undercurrent of something else. The man did not seem pleased with the squad's arrival here.

Neither did the rest of the force. Although the initial shock had passed, and the various police officers had resumed their regular work, the little glances and whispered exchanges around them spoke volumes.

They were not welcome here.

Adam glanced sideways at Major Williams, who stood confidently in the center of the room as though she was oblivious to it all. It had to be an act on her part. Next to her, Adam's brother Eric was constantly scanning their surroundings for any sign of a threat.

Even Cooper, the least intuitive of the team, had a subtle frown on his face as he stood there with his arms folded and back straightened. They were all aware of the vibe in the room, they just had different ways of showing it.

Thankfully, they didn't need to wait long before two men in suits approached. They were an odd pair. One, in his thirties, was almost as tall as Adam himself, and broad shouldered to boot. His shorter, older partner looked almost scrawny by comparison, even though he must have been about six feet tall himself and quite lean and athletic for his age.

"Major Williams. I'm Detective Nye, and this my partner, McMillan," the older detective spoke. "If your team could follow me into the conference room…"

The major nodded and gestured at everyone to follow the two men.

Adam couldn't stop staring at the younger detective, McMillan. He might have guessed the man was one of them: a shifter. If only Adam's nose wasn't telling him otherwise.

As soon as the team made it into the conference room, the two detectives started their briefing. From their body language, it was abundantly clear that they did not welcome Alpha Squad's help.

The way they presented the case, starting with images of mutilated livestock, progressing to a man and a woman—both torn to shreds—and finally ending with close-ups of the last victim who had been discovered only this afternoon, made it obvious that they were aiming for maximum shock value.

Adam couldn't deny that the photographs made an impact. He had not seen anything like it in his whole life.

"That makes three human deaths in total so far, all killed in the same brutal fashion. As you can imagine, we are looking carefully at the inhabitants of the local refugee camp," the older detective concluded.

Adam's body grew tense at the man's final statement.

Major Williams stepped up to the white board with the photographs. "We do not wish to step on anyone's toes, but we expect to be kept in the loop throughout this investigation. Any evidence you find, share it with us. We will do the same."

The two detectives exchanged a dark look. Finally, the chief inspector stepped in. "That will be all. I'm sure you want to get home to your families."

The older detective nodded and headed out, while the other one lingered in the door just a bit longer.

"We will need space to work. I would be very grateful if you could arrange for that," the major addressed the chief inspector.

"As you might have noticed, increased manpower coming in from the Metropolitan Police to help out with this investigation means we are a bit short on space ourselves. I will need until morning to work something out." The chief inspector nodded at Major Williams and folded his arms.

The message was clear. Nothing would happen until the following day.

Major Williams and Eric exchanged a look and seemed to come to an understanding without even speaking a word. The latter turned toward the rest of the team, including Adam.

"We will leave the local police to it for the evening and come back fresh in the morning," Eric said.

Adam frowned. It was unlike either Major Williams or Eric to just accept it when they were being pushed aside. Then again, it wasn't for him to question their orders either. He shrugged and took the lead out of the conference room, then crossed the room they had waited in previously.

Again, all the policemen and women present, as well as any other bystanders, stared at Adam and the rest of the task force suspiciously. They only seemed to resume their normal activity once they all had their backs turned and were almost out the door.

"Um… you can leave from the back exit if you like," the young man from reception spoke up as they almost passed him by, pointing to the other door behind him.

The major nodded and changed direction. Before they knew it they were outside, at the backside of the police station. The protesters' chants that had greeted them upon their arrival could still be heard, but they were a safe distance away and out of view.

"Apologies if this is out of line, but we're not actually

heading to the inn just yet, are we?" Bentley broke his silence.

It was clear to Adam that the former Special Forces man had reached the limits of his patience.

"Of course not, Bentley. But it's obvious that these people are not in a mood to help us. Whatever we do here, we'll have to do it on our own," Major Williams said. She tapped a few numbers into her phone and held it up to her ear. "Callahan, please bring the car around to the back of the station."

"Where to, then?" Adam asked.

Major Williams looked up and smiled briefly.

"The scene of the crime, of course," she said.

CHAPTER TWO

Felicity Weir had a lot on her plate. She had just returned home after spending all day at the shifter camp, making sure the new arrivals from the continent found their bearings, and she was beat. Almost every day at the camp was a struggle. The way the management ran the place was so inefficient, Felicity wondered how they ever achieved anything at all.

Just as she sat down on the sofa of her modest apartment, her phone was ringing again. *No rest for the wicked.*

The caller's number was withheld, but that was hardly unusual these days. Lately she'd been getting more phone calls from people she didn't know than her own family.

"Hello?" she answered.

There was a pause, but then finally, a familiar voice started to speak. "He's been at it again."

Felicity grabbed her notepad and a pen and readied herself. This man, whoever he was, had been giving her anonymous tips for the better part of a fortnight.

"More cattle?" she asked.

"I wish it were so. No, another human death this time, I'm afraid."

Felicity stopped scribbling. This was bad. The third murder in just over a week; this was sure to create a panic.

"Same M.O.?" she asked.

"We—they had to fingerprint him to determine his identity. He was mauled beyond recognition."

Felicity bit her lip. Ever since the secret Alliance had fallen apart, and their leader, Adrian Blacke, had been arrested by the human government, she had been drifting without any purpose. The incoming refugees gave her something to focus on, but she'd never expected for things to turn this ugly. Someone out there was intent on making all shifters look bad. That was the only explanation that made sense to her. The families she worked with every day at the camp were just as terrified about the new status quo as the locals in town were. They were honest, hard-working, and just trying to keep themselves and their families out of harm's way. None of them seemed capable of murder.

"Where?" she asked.

The man went on to explain the circumstances under which the body was discovered in some woods on the outskirts of town. The crime scene was just a moderate walk away from the shifter camp. Once he went quiet, Felicity knew that was all she was going to get out of him.

"Thank you. I will keep an eye out," Felicity said, then ended the call.

This was how her arrangement with the mysterious caller worked. She couldn't be sure how he'd found out about her, but in a small town like Sevenoaks, people liked to talk. And her presence in the camp had been a topic for speculation for many, until someone or other inevitably put two-and-two together and figured it out.

Felicity Weir was a bear shifter. She could pin-point the exact timing when the locals discovered this fact. The change in how everyone acted around her had been abrupt.

But Felicity had kept a level head. She had never planned on revealing her identity to the world like those people in the New Alliance had done some months ago on television. But she could understand their motivation. Still, they had made life much more difficult for everyone in her shoes. Shifter folk who had been living in secret among the human population all their lives and who now no longer knew how to deal with their new reality.

Should one come out and risk being ostracized by former friends and acquaintances? Or was it best to continue following the old ways, hoping that one's secret was never exposed?

Felicity felt strongly about her community and her species. The most important thing to her was to help her people and make a difference somehow. In a way, she had made her choice the day she walked into that refugee camp to offer her support to the newcomers.

But this... Felicity stared down at the words she'd hastily scribbled onto the notepad.

Murder. Human male. Mauled beyond recognition. Deer Park.

As soon as the media got wind of this, tempers would

flare yet again, just as they had done after the previous attacks. Things were obviously escalating. At first, when only animals had been harmed, even Felicity wondered if some of the younger shifters from the camp had decided to go for a hunt and gotten carried away.

All shifters, herself included, had certain instincts and urges, after all. Hunting was not an uncommon activity among her kind.

But as soon as human victims started turning up, she changed her mind. Why would someone give up his or her entire life to come here and then cause trouble by attacking the local population? It just didn't make sense. And such violence, too. The particulars of the three murders turned her stomach.

She sighed and sat back with her eyes closed.

Who could have done this? Would it ever end?

After staying like that for a few more minutes, she tried to shake off the growing dread in her heart and recompose herself. It had been hours since her last meal; the volunteer work had kept her too busy all day.

It would be too easy to just call for a pizza, but she forced herself into action anyway and headed for the kitchen. There she switched on the radio and waited for the music to do its job.

Instead, voices started to fill the small kitchen. A panel discussion about exactly the topic she had wanted to find distraction from.

Rather than listening in on the heated debate about whether or not shifters were a threat to society, she switched the device off again and quickly made herself a sandwich. No way would she find rest after this latest tip. She ate in a rush, then put on an extra layer of warm clothes and headed out the door. The police might have left the crime scene by now, giving her time to inspect it and perhaps find a few clues human eyes would have overlooked.

Felicity carefully scanned her surroundings as she entered the Deer Park. According to the information she had received, the crime scene was supposedly situated along the western side of the park.

Every so often, she stopped and listened for any unusual activity, but could not detect any. All was calm. The only noises she could hear were those of the local animals going about their evening routines.

Twilight had descended on the park, meaning that this was the time of peak activity for the local deer as well as certain other wildlife. The herd was moving in the opposite direction of the area where the crime scene was supposed to be, meaning Felicity soon found herself surrounded by silence.

She approached the area that the police had taped off, all the while looking over her shoulder to ensure she was not being followed or watched.

Only when she was certain that she was all alone did she approach the tape boundary and crawl underneath to get a closer look at the scene.

She was light on her feet like only a shifter could be, and made sure she did not disturb anything.

The body had been taken away quite some time ago, but the scent of blood still clung to the moist air. This was where the victim was attacked and had died, she was certain of it. There was blood evidence all over the trees that stood guard around the unfortunate man's last resting place, which in her mind ruled out the possibility for it being a body dump.

The previous attack sites had been similar. The bodies were never moved, they were just left wherever they had fallen.

If she was still considering the possibility of a shifter hunting party gone awry, the fact that the bodies were never moved seemed to prove the opposite.

Predators tend to retreat to a safe place to consume their prey. They wouldn't be this brazen.

Felicity took position right next to the bloodstained moss where the body must have fallen and looked back to where she had just hiked in from. This part of the park wasn't at all secure. The trees were loosely planted, with large of gaps in between. And the underbrush had been cleared only last season. If Felicity had to pick a spot to tear apart freshly caught prey, this would not have been it.

Still, she couldn't very well tell the local police that. They knew too little about shifter behavior to take her concerns seriously. To them, she would just be *one of the enemy*, trying to dissuade them from investigating a serious threat based on speculation and vague theories.

No, she would have to find out the truth on her own.

It was almost dark now, though that didn't bother her too much. She was able to see just fine in this light.

As much as it repelled her, she got down onto her haunches and carefully inspected the blood-soaked ground. Moss, pine needles, and fallen leaves from the earlier shedding deciduous trees in the park probably made this a challenging environment for the police forensics to do their work. At least that was what Felicity assumed.

Her eyes were able to focus on every detail, even the smallest particles mixed in with the loose soil, if only she could stand the stench of blood long enough.

In the end, something did catch her eye. A glimmer of something shiny stood out against all the dull organic matter. It was a tiny metal fragment.

She carefully picked it up and held it up to her nose. Blood.

Could this be a piece of whatever weapon had caused all this damage?

Felicity retrieved a resealable bag from her pocket and dropped the splinter into it, sealing it tightly before stuffing it into her jacket pocket. She got up again and couldn't help but shake her head at the whole scenario. If someone had told her a couple of months ago that she would find herself in the woods, investigating a crime scene and securing evidence in spare sandwich bags from her kitchen, she probably would have laughed.

And yet here she was.

Her moment of contemplation did not last. She was startled by footsteps and voices approaching from the east; a group of people—humans, judging from the heaviness of their footsteps—was heading toward her.

She quickly checked the area to ensure she hadn't left anything behind and crouched underneath the boundary tape again. Then she broke into a jog heading in the opposite direction: west.

The humans were far away enough that they shouldn't have heard her, and still, she thought she heard rustling behind her. Someone was following her!

That was when her instincts took over; within a split second, she transformed and broke into a sprint, heading as far away from the crime scene as she possibly could.

She couldn't be sure exactly who was after her; the headwind meant that she couldn't catch her chaser's scent. Still, someone that fast had to be super-human. Perhaps it was just one of the refugees who had wandered into the woods for an evening stroll. Perhaps it was nothing.

Or perhaps, it was the murderer…

Felicity's instincts did not allow her to take any

chances. Even if it was nothing, she still did not wish to be discovered tampering with evidence of a crime. That would only raise questions.

And so she did not look back, just went hell for leather straight across the park until she could no longer hear anyone behind her. The strange presence that had followed her must have given up. Perhaps he wasn't fast or motivated enough to maintain that kind of pace. Either way, she was finally alone again.

She was safe.

Rather than double back and risk running into this person again, she took the long way home.

Although she had left the latest murder scene with more questions rather than answers, something felt different now. There was someone else out there whose motivations she could not yet understand.

Combine that with the growing protests of the local human population to close the camp and deport all its residents… and the pressure was on. One way or another, Felicity had to figure out who really was behind all these attacks before something even worse happened.

CHAPTER THREE

Adam wasn't sure how long he had been running through the woods when he stopped. What was he even doing?

They had entered the park, looking for the crime scene the two detectives at the police station had told them about, when some activity up ahead had stirred his suspicions and compelled him to give chase. He hadn't even taken the time to alert Eric or the rest of the team what exactly he was up to, he'd just gone for it.

And now, he was probably a mile away from where he started. How was he going to explain this? Something had awoken his animal instincts and compelled him to run. What—or rather, who—he'd been running after smelled like a bear, but not like any he'd ever met before.

There was something different about this scent, something… tempting.

He scratched his head and turned back again, tracking his as well as the other shifter's footprints to where all of this had begun.

Even though it was already quite dark, he could clearly see the taped up crime scene in the distance. But his team wasn't investigating the crime scene, they were about ten feet away from it, leaning over something on the ground.

"Where did you rush off to, soldier?" Major Williams demanded.

Adam averted his gaze from hers. Ordinarily, he did not appreciate being questioned like that, but she was unquestionably in charge of this unit. A lot had changed ever since he'd joined Alpha Squad, even his attitude. "Ma'am, I was chasing an intruder."

He glanced at Eric, who had his arms folded. The other team members stood by in silence. Bentley glaring as usual, whereas Cooper—for lack of a better description—just looked vacant. Blackwood wasn't even looking at Adam; instead, he was still focusing on that something on the ground they had all been studying moments ago.

"Bro, I'm telling you, there was somebody here," Adam insisted.

"I understand. But you can't just run off like that. We're a team, remember?" Eric said.

Adam sighed and nodded. His older brother was right. Teamwork wasn't his forte.

"What's that?" Adam asked, pointing at the thing Blackwood had been staring at.

"Looks like a shred of clothing," Blackwood said, leaning down to pick it up.

"Wait!" the major snapped, causing Blackwood to flinch back. "Remember your training; police procedures 101. This may not be part of the crime scene, technically, but it's still evidence."

Blackwood relaxed again and retrieved a pen from one of the pockets on his technical vest. He picked up the fabric by balancing it on the end of the pen and held it up at face height.

All three shifters on the team leaned in closer to inspect the item.

"Don't tell me you're going to sniff the perp out!" Bentley protested.

"Whatever works," Eric said.

Adam found himself lost for words. That scent. It was so much stronger on this piece of fabric, but it unmistakably belonged to the bear he'd just chased. He found himself almost overwhelmed by it. Floral notes complemented a rich, warm, inviting base scent that reminded him of a cinnamon roll fresh out of the oven.

"Definitely female," Blackwood remarked.

"I agree," Eric said.

"Why on earth would some woman be snooping around a murder scene in the dark?" the major wondered aloud.

"Not just any woman," Eric said.

"Bear shifter," Adam finally spoke up.

The three humans—Bentley, Cooper, and Major Williams—all turned their heads in his direction.

Was it what he said? Or how he said it? Had they caught on to the strange effect this female bear's scent had on him?

Adam pressed his lips together and waited for someone else to speak. After running off without warning on their very first field assignment, the last thing he needed was to make an even bigger fool of himself.

Eric broke the silence. "It's not so dark for us. She would have been able to see just fine."

"Ah, yes, of course," the major mumbled.

"Well, this is all highly suspicious. We've got bodies that have been mauled by something with large, sharp teeth, and now a bear shifter woman tampering with the crime scene." Bentley cleared his throat. "It's got to be our suspect, surely!"

Adam frowned. That was a bit of a stretch.

"That's one theory," Eric said.

"We'll investigate all possibilities," the major said. "But just in case this is our murderer, then we must follow protocol. Under no circumstance are any of you—that includes you, Adam—to go after this individual on your own. We don't know what she's capable of. It's too risky."

Adam frowned again. She'd been faster than him, sure, but she'd had a significant head start, and she'd shifted, which explained the torn clothing. Although a confrontation with a fellow shifter wasn't without risks, he couldn't accept that she posed a threat to him, or anyone else. Perhaps she had another reason to be here tonight.

But voicing out his doubts would just get Bentley riled up again. Adam decided to keep his thoughts to himself.

"Blackwood, secure that piece of fabric as per protocol. And let's actually investigate what we came here to see, the crime scene." Major Williams pointed her flashlight back in the direction of the police tape.

ALPHA SQUAD: FRIENDS AND FOES

The bright light was a bit distracting. Adam, as well Eric and Blackwood, would have found it easier to see in whatever natural light there was. Of course, the humans weren't able to function that way.

Despite having trained together, there was still a lot Adam had to get used to now that he was working so closely with members of another species.

They spent about an hour in the park, investigating, discussing, and taking notes and samples. But the more they talked about the case, the more obvious it became to Adam that Bentley had already made up his mind. The man clearly didn't believe in coincidences.

The shifters, Adam included, took a more pragmatic approach. Rather than point the finger at one of their own, they wished for more information.

"She's definitely been here, within the tape boundary," Eric said.

Adam and Blackwood nodded in agreement. *But why?*

Bentley scoffed. "As I've told you. She's the one. Though you lot being able to smell her around the place is not going to do us much good as evidence."

Adam rolled his eyes.

"We should probably examine the body," Blackwood suggested. "Get a better sense of what we're dealing with."

The others paused for a moment. It was a logical request, but Adam wasn't keen to get too close to a dead body. The pictures they'd seen at the police station were plenty graphic for his taste.

"Excellent thinking, Blackwood," Major Williams said. "I will put in a request with Chief Inspector Huddersfield tomorrow morning."

Adam glanced at Eric, who showed no sign of worry or distaste at the prospect of getting close to a viciously mutilated murder victim. Then again, Eric famously never showed his emotions.

Fine. We'll suck it up and carry on, then, Adam thought.

Whoever the woman in the woods was, perhaps she wouldn't be anywhere near that squeamish. She's voluntarily wandered around a bloody crime scene by herself, right until Adam and the rest of the team arrived. He wouldn't be a coward about it either.

Major Williams rounded everyone up. "Let's call it a night. Tomorrow the investigation *really* begins."

"Yes, Ma'am," the squad responded in unison.

Together, they marched back to where they'd left the Land Rover. Private Callahan had either not moved at all in the time they were in the woods, or had hearing as good as any shifter, because she was in position behind the wheel already.

"To the inn," Major Williams instructed.

Callahan nodded and turned the key, causing the old engine to cough to life.

It didn't take them long to pile into the back. Soon after, the vehicle started its short drive to their stop for the night: an old farmhouse that had been converted into a pub and inn. This wasn't half bad.

The scents emanating from the dining hall were promising as well. After a whole day on the move, Adam's stomach could not wait to sample all that this place had to offer.

A quick glance around the rest of the team suggested everyone, including the humans, felt the same.

———•———

The hearty meal put Adam in a calmer, more reflective mood. He found himself sitting in a big leather armchair around the fireplace at the far end of the pub. His brother Eric sat opposite in the other chair.

"It's not quite what I expected," Adam said.

"What is?"

"This mission."

Eric nodded. "Well, I suppose few things in life are as we expect them to be." He glanced across the room at the major, who had been deep in conversation with Private Callahan. Adam frowned when he noticed the major pause and looked up in Eric's direction. More of that nonverbal communication stuff he'd noticed earlier in the day.

"What's going on between you and the major?" Adam blurted out.

Eric blinked a few times and pressed his lips together as though he had been caught in the act.

"Bro, don't you tell me it's nothing. I have eyes," Adam

insisted. His brother had a hard time sharing, but Adam was ready to pry him open once and for all.

"Don't you say a word to the others," Eric spoke in a low growl.

Adam rolled his eyes. "As if. Now, spill!"

Eric stared him down in silence for a moment, until he finally started to explain. "Fine. We're mates."

That made perfect sense, but the revelation still came as a bit of a shock to Adam. "Mates? Bro, when did that happen?"

Eric shrugged. "I could feel it from the beginning. Just like the stories go."

Adam sat back and scratched his chin. "When we saw her at the motorway services?"

Eric nodded.

"Wow. And nobody else knows?" Adam asked.

Eric gave him one of those disapproving big brother looks. "Of course not. How do you think Bentley would take it? Or bloody General Stone, who—"

Adam's eyes widened. "General Stone, who, what?"

Eric shook his head. "No. None of your business. And anyway, it's not important. The main thing is, we're a couple, and nobody can know about it, at least for now."

Adam did his best not to stare at Major Williams from across the pub. He'd never thought of her that way. The woman wasn't someone to mess with; the way she ran the squad demonstrated as much. And to think that she was basically like his sister-in-law? It was a lot to take in.

ALPHA SQUAD: FRIENDS AND FOES

"But you knew it immediately, like, when you saw her?"

Eric frowned at him. "Why are you so interested in this?"

"Just… no particular reason," Adam said.

Eric squinted at him, like he could see right through his lie. Of course Adam had a very specific reason for asking these questions. The scent of the woman he'd chased through the park had had a very odd effect on him. Could something similar be going on here as what had happened between Major Williams and his very own brother?

"I suppose it was a combination of things. Seeing her, her scent, a kind of magnetism between us. It's tough to explain."

Adam nodded. That was already a lot more information than he could have hoped for. Bottom line: you knew it when you felt it. There was only one solution: Adam had to find the woman who had been in the woods today and figure out exactly how he felt once he saw her face-to-face. Only then would he find out the whole truth about her.

CHAPTER FOUR

Felicity was still on edge when she made it back home. Being chased halfway across Deer Park by a strange superhuman was something she hadn't planned for when she'd headed out to see the crime scene.

Her private investigation was becoming a lot more intense and risky than she'd foreseen. But the refugees were counting on her. And the more bodies turned up, the worse the consequences for them would be.

She didn't have a choice but to soldier on; they had nobody else looking out for them.

Felicity changed out of her torn clothes and took a deep breath. Like most bears, she was a loner by nature and normally, she was content spending time on her own. But not tonight.

Ever since her big secret had come out, she had lost the one childhood friend who she'd still kept in touch with since growing up, a human named Joy. That meant that the only people she could reach out to were her parents, who still lived in the same house she'd grown up in. She couldn't tell them everything she was up to, obviously, as that would only worry them, but it was better than no company at all.

That was where she would go, before the walls of her small flat threatened to close in on her and the silence became deafening.

When she locked the front door again, she found that her hands were trembling slightly. It had been a very long, very trying day.

Just as she got into her car, she was interrupted by her phone. Anonymous, again.

Felicity frowned, then answered. It was highly unusual to get two tips in one day.

Sure enough, it was the same voice on the other end. Her mysterious tipster had called once more.

"The government has sent in a brand new task force to investigate the deaths. Alpha Squad."

Felicity rummaged in the glove box for a pen and paper and scribbled the particulars down. Alpha Squad. What a weird name. It sounded more like a fictional unit than a real one. If anyone other than this very serious caller had mentioned the name to her, she might have thought it was a joke.

"What are they? What's their purpose?" Felicity asked.

The caller did not respond immediately.

"They report to the Ministry of Shifter Affairs."

Oh God, that wasn't good, was it? That meant that even on the highest levels, the government felt that these deaths were linked to the shifter camp.

Felicity rested her head on her free hand on top of the steering wheel, but that did nothing to stop her heart from sinking.

"Have they taken over the investigation?" she asked, her voice flat and listless.

"It's a collaboration. Kent police are unhappy about the intrusion."

Felicity nodded. She wasn't happy either.

"Thank you," she said.

The line went dead.

So her instincts had been spot on. Something *had* changed today, and the odds were further stacked against her. Now she definitely needed a change of scenery.

Luckily, Felicity's childhood home was only a short drive away on the edge of town. As she pulled into the long driveway, the subtle glow of the lights filtering through the curtains in the kitchen filled her with a sense of nostalgia. No matter what she got up to all day, here she felt safe.

Felicity stuck her key in the lock and opened the front door, only to be greeted almost immediately by her mother, who came rushing into the entrance hall to see who it was.

"Sweetheart. What a pleasant surprise!" Felicity was immediately engulfed in a big hug. "Your father's inside watching the TV. Come in, make yourself comfortable!"

Felicity smiled and found that her eyes were starting to get a bit moist. It certainly was good to be home. Hopefully she could forget about everything, just for a little while.

"Thanks, Mom," she said as she removed her coat and hung it up on the rack. Then she followed her inside.

"Hi, Dad!" Felicity called out once she made it into the living room.

Her father turned his head briefly and grunted an acknowledgment before diverting his attention back at the flickering images on the screen in front of him.

"Can I get you something to eat? You look tired. Have you been sleeping enough?"

Felicity smiled again, but didn't respond. Of course she was tired, exhausted even.

"Oh dear, your hair! You look terrible!" her mom added.

Felicity stood by awkwardly while getting some dry leaves removed from her dark brown locks. This was how her home visits usually started. A whole lot of questions from her mom, a syllable or two from her dad, until things settled down and she could relax a bit.

"Sit down," her mom said. "I'll make you something."

Felicity did as she was told, as her mom continued to chatter away about this and that. This was why she was here. For the company. For a little slice of a simpler life, before people found out about shifters living in their midst.

Felicity watched from the small breakfast table as her mom flitted around the kitchen, heating up some leftover stew and pouring it into a big porcelain bowl. Nothing much had changed in this house. The kitchen still sported the green and brown retro tiles that had been so popular in the '70s. Even the pots and pans her mom was using were still the same.

The only change in this house over the four years since Felicity had moved out on her own were that its inhabitants had grown just a bit older and grayer than before.

Still, Felicity's parents weren't *that* old yet. Her dad still had a few years to go until retirement, and her mom was as energetic as she'd always been. In the summer, she would spend the entire day tending to the large garden that surrounded the house without ever growing tired.

Though the longer Felicity watched, the more she felt like something *was* different. Some vibe had crept into this house that hadn't been there before. Perhaps it was just that *she herself* felt different tonight. The dirty politics at the shifter camp, plus the murder investigation, were really getting to her.

"Here you go, darling."

Felicity watched her mom put down the bowl and a couple of toasted slices of bread in front of her, before taking a seat on the chair opposite.

"Thanks," she said, as she picked up a spoon and leaned across to inhale the various aromas of the rich lamb stew. Just like in the good old days.

She blew on the first bite, then closed her eyes when she tasted it. Her body had been craving proper food like this earlier. Not a sandwich or some other small snack. This was the real deal.

It wasn't long before she noticed her mother's eyes still boring into her.

"What is it, Mom?" she asked, putting the spoon down on the table.

"This work you do… it's taking its toll on you. I can see it."

"You know I'm just trying to help our people, right? I mean, someone's got to do it!" Felicity argued.

Her mother nodded. "It's a noble cause, darling. But you're putting yourself at risk out there. Your father agrees."

Felicity cocked her head to the side. She hadn't really talked about any of this stuff with her parents; she didn't want to worry them. But they had a way of noticing when she felt down.

"These people have nobody else," Felicity said.

"You can't carry the weight of the world on your shoulders. We were worried about you back when you joined the Alliance as well. And the truth is, the world is different now. More dangerous."

Felicity felt herself grow defensive. Things were plenty dangerous back when Adrian Blacke was in charge of the Alliance. Most humans might not have known about shifters yet, but their main enemy, the Sons of Domnall, did. And the Alliance itself wasn't so innocent either when they thought someone had broken *the rules*. Her parents had luckily been shielded from most of this stuff, so they had no way of knowing.

It was probably best to keep it that way, so she bit her lip instead of speaking out.

"Darling, we just want you to promise us that you'll be careful." Her mother placed her hand on top of Felicity's.

"Of course, Mom. I promise," Felicity mumbled. She would be careful, but she would still continue her work as well as her investigation. She simply didn't have any other choice.

"And perhaps you might want to think about the future as well. You're not getting any younger, you know," her mom added.

Felicity frowned. Not this again. Perhaps if she ignored it, they could move on to a less awkward topic.

A loud crashing sound interrupted the silence in the kitchen, causing Felicity to jump up. Broken glass covered the floor, and a brick lay in the center of it.

"What on earth?" Felicity called out and charged toward the windows to see who had thrown the brick.

Her mother gestured at her to come back. "Leave it. It's just some kids, probably."

"Kids? What kind of kids throw bricks into people's homes? It could have hit you or Dad, and then what? You could have got seriously hurt!" Felicity ranted.

She marched through the lobby and straight out the front door.

"Who's out there? Show yourselves!" she shouted.

There was no answer; in fact, there was no sound at all except a couple of pairs of distant footsteps, running away. Whoever the culprits were, they were long gone.

"I don't believe it," Felicity grumbled to herself as she went back inside the house.

"Someone threw a brick through the window," she complained to her dad, who was still sitting in his arm chair in front of the TV.

"You should see the filth they wrote on the garage door. Your mother spent all day cleaning it off yesterday," her dad remarked.

"What? Why didn't you tell me?" Felicity demanded.

She marched back into the kitchen, where her mother had begun collecting the broken glass.

"You didn't tell me people have been harassing you and vandalizing the house!" Felicity said.

No response.

"Leave it, I'll clear it up," Felicity insisted and got down on her knees to pick up some of the larger pieces of glass.

"We didn't want to worry you, darling. You have enough on your plate as it is."

Felicity was stunned. Whereas earlier she had found herself teary eyed with nostalgia, it was anger and guilt that tugged at her emotions now. This was *her* fault, wasn't it? As soon as the town had found out about her true nature, it wasn't enough that she'd been shunned. People had taken it upon themselves to terrorize her parents too.

It was so unfair. She was only trying to help people, not hurt them! And why her parents? They were innocent in all this. If anyone had a problem with what Felicity was up to, they ought to confront her directly, not take it out on a couple of near-retirees!

"Darling, don't worry about it. It's only a window," her mother said. "It was old anyway. The frame was starting to rot. We'll get some new double glazing fitted now. It's about time we made a few improvements to the house."

But no matter what her mother said, Felicity couldn't hold back the tears anymore. By the time she had finished brushing every last bit of glass into an old dustpan, she found that her face was completely wet. She was drained. This entire day had gotten the best of her, and the bricked window was just the last straw.

When she sat back down at the table, the kitchen was a good ten degrees colder. Gusts of wind were entering through the now non-existent window, causing the curtains to billow violently.

"I'll get someone to fix it tomorrow." Felicity sniffled and wiped her eyes with the back of her hand.

"It's fine. We'll handle it. You just take care of yourself," her mother said as she too sat back down. "It's a bit gusty, isn't it? Maybe we ought to head into the lounge, what do you say?"

Felicity nodded and pushed her chair back again.

"Remember that hat you used to love when you were

little?" her mom said, with a little smile playing on her lips.

"The crocodile one?" Felicity asked.

Her mom nodded. "You wore it even in the spring, even when it was much too warm out and your hair would get sweaty underneath it."

"It was a cute hat," Felicity said.

"Yes, it was."

"What made you think of that?" Felicity asked.

"Oh, you know. Your cheeks were getting flushed from the cold wind coming in. I thought how funny it would be if you had your hat."

Felicity shook her head. Sometimes her mom came up with the weirdest things. Despite everything, a little smile crept over her lips too. It had been a good decision to drop by here tonight, after all.

At least now she knew about her parents' troubles. At least she could try to help somehow.

CHAPTER FIVE

―――◆―――

The whole squad was up bright and early.

Adam didn't know about the others, especially the humans, but the weeks of intense training had at least changed him and his brother forever. Bear shifters weren't known to be early risers. It generally took them a while—and a whole lot of very sweet coffee—to get going.

Nowadays though, Adam found that getting up early had become somewhat of a habit. He almost didn't mind it anymore.

Having to get up and get ready to leave the inn by eight was almost a luxury.

The entire team stood by and listened as Major Williams made her first phone call of the day; she called Chief Inspector Huddersfield in order to get access to the body that had been recovered from the woods the other day.

From the major's expressions throughout the conversation, it was obvious that the local police was still being a stick in the mud.

"I understand it's early, but the sooner we inspect the body, the sooner we can start making inquiries," the major said. "And we do still need some space to work out of, if it's not too much to ask."

Adam couldn't hear what was being said on the other

end. For a moment he envied Eric, who was probably participating in the entire conversation non-verbally himself. There was obviously more to the squad and its leadership than they had been led to believe. The remark Eric let slip about General Stone was proof of the same.

"Very well, we will be at the mortuary at ten," Major Williams conceded. She was still frowning when she hung up the phone and turned to face the squad.

Adam checked his watch, they'd better not be hanging around here for two hours. They had important work to do.

"The local police are going to take some time arranging our visit with the medical examiner. We will follow other lines of inquiry in the meantime." Major Williams signaled Private Callahan, who climbed into the cab of the Land Rover and started the engine.

"We're heading to the refugee camp to question some people there. Perhaps we'll get lucky and find someone who's willing to talk," the major said.

Adam was strangely relieved that their encounter with the murder victim had been postponed, but he also felt a little awkward about heading to the shifter camp. He hadn't specifically followed the shifter refugee crisis in the news, but the coverage was so intense lately it was impossible not to be aware of it.

Shifters, sometimes entire families of them, displaced from their homes and forced to find a safe haven elsewhere... It wasn't all that easy uprooting yourself and adjusting to a new place; he'd done it once himself when he was little and his parents had moved Eric and him to East London. It wasn't easy adjusting to a different school and making new friends, when you felt like an outsider.

And these people weren't just moving to a new city within the same country; they had moved across borders. Did they even speak English?

And if they did have a killer in their midst, that made things infinitely more complicated.

As their vehicle passed through the small town center of Sevenoaks to get to the shifter camp, which was located on the same side of town as yesterday's crime scene, it was obvious that the protests they had witnessed the day before had left their mark.

The only people about this time of day were commuters heading to work, but banners left behind by the protesters lined High Street. Posters calling for the closure of the camp could be found hanging in almost every shop window.

Sevenoaks was close to hitting breaking point.

The team did not speak much throughout the drive; each of the guys in the back just quietly observed what they could from whichever window they had access to.

When they pulled into an overgrown drive on the outskirts of town, Adam felt a change come over him. He'd been apprehensive about coming here before, worried that it would be uncomfortable seeing his people struggle. But now something, some presence, seemed to be pulling him in closer.

Resistance was futile.

He grew impatient watching as Major Williams negotiated with the guard at the gate. The urge to get out of the vehicle and proceed on foot came over him again, just like it had done the night before. But this time, he managed to control himself.

Adam breathed a sigh of relief when Major Williams had seemingly come to some understanding with the guard and gotten back into the cab.

Soon, the gate was opened for them and their vehicle started to move again.

The surroundings of the camp were nice enough: quaint countryside as far as the eye could see.

Of course, from the back of the Land Rover, Adam could not see what lay ahead.

It was only when they got off that Adam got a proper view of what the shifter refugee camp actually looked like. It wasn't as bad as he'd thought. It wasn't even that big. Makeshift houses made out of shipping containers were positioned in a circular layout around a central square. At the most, there were about two dozen of these temporary living quarters, along with a bigger structure that looked like some kind of administrative building.

There was quite a bit of activity going on. People going about their morning routine, kids playing in the grass.

"Let's split up," Major Williams said, then she signaled Private Callahan. "Collect your official ID badges and form two groups. Half of you will join me as I talk to whoever is in charge here, half of you canvass the camp and talk to the residents. Eric will take the lead on that."

Adam glanced over at his brother. He knew whose team he wanted to be on.

It didn't take long for the group to split up. As expected, the divide was clean; humans in one group, shifters in the other. It was the shifters who were better equipped to talk to the residents of the camp anyway, and that was exactly what they were going to do.

"Right. Blackwood," Eric started. "You talk to any wolves you encounter. These houses to the left seem like a good start." Adam suppressed a smile. Eric had attempted to be tactful, but Adam could clearly catch the smell of wet dog in the air. The houses Eric had pointed out were definitely inhabited by wolves, there was no doubt about it.

Blackwood nodded and did as he was told without comment.

"Now, Adam, we'll divide the remaining houses among the two of us. Let's see how we get on, what do you say?"

Adam rested his hands on his hips and surveyed the camp. That pull he'd felt the moment they'd neared the camp was stronger now. And it was calling him off to the wooded area behind the houses. Should he risk it?

"Sure, bro. I'll take the row at the back," Adam said.

ALPHA SQUAD: FRIENDS AND FOES

Eric nodded. "We'll reconvene here once we're done."

Whew, it seemed Eric hadn't suspected anything.

Adam returned the gesture and marched off resolutely in the direction the strange sensation he was feeling seemed to be originating from. Before skipping past the houses he was meant to canvass, he checked over his shoulder once more, but Eric was nowhere to be seen. This was his chance.

They stood face-to-face and just stared at each other. Adam had nothing to say. Apparently, neither did the female. Still, the silence did not feel awkward; it was as though they were getting to know each other, just by observing.

He watched her as she pushed a lock of her brown wavy hair behind her ear and continued to look up at him. A glow appeared in her eyes that seemed perfectly matched with the warmth that seemed to fill his chest. This pull he felt, this connection, it was mutual.

This was what Eric had been talking about.

Still, there was a lot of distance between them, at least figuratively. Adam could not hear her thoughts. Did that mean they weren't truly mates? His heart insisted on the opposite.

She was *the one*, he would bet his life on it.

He cleared his throat, but she spoke up before he had

the chance.

"It was you in the woods last night," she said. Her voice had a warmth, as well as a rawness, that tugged at his emotions. So this was what his woman sounded like.

Adam nodded. "I'm sorry if I spooked you. Something came over me and I just had to chase you." He pressed his lips together. It sounded so silly now that he'd said it out loud.

The woman smiled briefly and averted her gaze. "It was a bit unnerving, I must admit."

"Adam? Where are you?" Eric's voice called out for him from the other side of the woods. He was quite far away still, but it made him nervous nonetheless. The last thing he needed right now was to be found by the rest of the team.

"Your colleagues?" the woman asked.

"Yeah. We're meant to be canvassing the camp, questioning people about those attacks," Adam responded without much consideration. It didn't even occur to him to keep the woman in the dark about their purpose here.

She frowned. "You think it's one of the residents? One of our own?"

Adam paused. He wasn't quite sure what to think. "I have to tell you, some of the team were suspicious about your presence at the crime scene. You left behind a scrap of fabric right next to it when you ran. I'm so sorry."

"Great." The woman folded her arms and shook her head in dismay.

ALPHA SQUAD: FRIENDS AND FOES

This was his fault. His decision to run after her had caused her to leave behind evidence of her presence at the crime scene. Somehow, he had to fix it, but how?

Adam glanced backward, looking for any indication that Eric was close to catching up with him, but there was no sign of movement in the trees and shrubs surrounding them.

"I'm going to talk to them. I'll straighten things out," he said, but his voice didn't sound convincing.

The woman cocked her head to the side. "Well, if you're here to figure out what really happened, that would sort things out anyway. I had nothing to do with the attacks."

"Of course not. I didn't mean to suggest—"

"I'm just trying to do the same thing. Find out what really happened."

Adam nodded. There was nothing left to be said. He believed her, obviously. For better or for worse. Hopefully she could see that his intentions were pure as well.

A rustling sound set off his protective instincts. It would only be a matter of time before Eric found him. And when he did, he'd have a lot of explaining to do as it was.

"You'd better go before my team gets here," Adam whispered. "It's best if they don't catch you. Just until I can sort things out."

The woman nodded. "I understand."

She stared into his eyes one more time, then turned away, readying herself for a sprint.

"Wait," Adam said.

The woman froze.

"What's your name?" he asked.

She glanced back at him with that same subtle smile playing on her lips that he'd seen earlier. "Felicity."

"I'm Adam," he said.

"Yeah, I figured."

She nodded at him once, then broke into a sprint. It was mesmerizing to look at. She was almost soundless as she darted away, zig-zagging through the trees.

Adam wasn't sure how long he'd stood there, gazing longingly in the direction where Felicity had fled to, when a heavy hand rested on his shoulder.

"Adam. What the hell?" Eric demanded.

Adam turned and averted his gaze. He'd ignored direct orders. Although his training had gone well, the ground reality of being part of this task force was a lot more difficult than he'd foreseen. Especially now that there were these complications to deal with.

Felicity. What a name. What a woman.

"Uh, I thought I heard something, so I came here to investigate."

Eric frowned, then his eyes narrowed. "That scent. The female from the crime scene!"

Adam shook his head and raised his hands in a calming motion. "Relax, bro. Let me explain!"

Eric folded his arms. "Fine. Explain!"

"She had nothing to do with it. She was investigating the crime scene just like we were."

"And you know this how?" Eric asked.

Adam pressed his lips together. All or nothing. Eric would know immediately if he was lying.

"I talked to her."

"You, what? After Janine—Major Williams ordered all of us not to approach this woman alone?" Eric exclaimed.

"It's okay. As I said, she had nothing to do with those crimes. Felicity's harmless."

"Felicity, huh?"

"Uh, yeah. Just—" Adam took a deep breath. "Just keep this to yourself for now, please, bro? I'll tell you everything when the time is right."

Eric frowned again. "I won't say anything to the team, for now. But you know there are no secrets between Janine and I."

Adam sighed. Of course. Perhaps soon there wouldn't be any secrets between Felicity and him either. But it was too early to say that out loud.

"Let's just continue canvassing the camp, what do you say?" Adam suggested.

"That's what you were meant to be doing in the first place."

"I know. I'm sorry, okay? Trust me, I have my reasons."

Eric stared at Adam for a few seconds; Adam stood his ground and stared back.

"Very well. I'll back off for now."

Adam nodded, relieved to have won this round. "Thanks, bro."

CHAPTER SIX

With Alpha Squad still snooping around the shifter camp, Felicity had no choice but to return home early. She couldn't risk getting caught, at least not while they thought she was a suspect.

The one hope she clung onto was that these newcomers seemed to be investigating the deaths on their own without getting much in the way of support from the local police. Assuming Adam was able to convince them of her innocence, she would have nothing to worry about.

Their encounter in the woods had been a very strange experience. Felicity wasn't sure what to make of it all. She'd hidden in the woods as soon as she saw the Army Land Rover pull into the camp, and he'd followed her immediately after.

She should have run, but unlike the previous night in the Deer Park, something told her to stick around. Now she was glad she had. There was something about him which made her want to trust his intentions.

But she couldn't put her finger on what it was exactly.

The look in his eyes? Those beautifully deep brown eyes…

Or was it something else? The strange magnetism she'd felt the moment she saw him approach? At that point, she couldn't have run even if she wanted to.

He was a peculiar man.

And something deep within herself made her want to be near him.

Now, in the safety of her car, she couldn't help but run through the short encounter again and again in her head.

Finally, she forced herself out of her daydream and turned the key. She would check in with her mom to see how she was holding up after last night's incident. Felicity still couldn't believe that someone would just throw a brick through their window. This town was going downhill fast. Tensions were rising.

Upon pulling into the quiet cul-de-sac upon which her childhood home stood, she was greeted by the flashing lights of police cars. Felicity's heart sank. Had the vandals taken a step further now? Were her parents all right?

The tires of her car screeched as she stopped abruptly along the curb near their house and raced up the lengthy driveway toward the door. She hadn't even bothered to take the keys out of the ignition or lock the car.

She burst through the door and into the house, still panting in panic.

"What's happened? Mom, are you all right? Where's Dad?" Felicity called out.

She froze when she saw two men in suits sitting in the couch, cups of tea in hand, with her mom leaning across to offer them biscuits from a serving tray.

"Darling! These gentlemen were just asking about you!" Her mom straightened herself and smiled briefly. Still,

Felicity could tell that something was wrong. "And your father is at work, where he should be."

Felicity tried to get her breathing under control and think about what to do. The hint of tension in her mother's expression told her to run. But that would just attract undue attention. Perhaps it was best to talk to the police and see what they were actually here for. They couldn't arrest her unless they actually had something on her, right?

"Hello, I'm Felicity Weir," she introduced herself.

The nearest of the two men, a gray-haired man, about six feet tall, stood up and shook her hand. "Detective Nye. This is my partner, Detective McMillan."

"Nice to meet you," Felicity mumbled. She nodded at the other, younger man who remained seated on the couch. Taller than his partner, and broader as well, even while seated, Detective McMillan was an imposing house guest.

There was something off about him. It was rare to see a human man of his stature and fitness level, except for gym nuts who rarely stopped working out. And yet, his scent was unmistakable. *Human.*

"Well, it's a happy coincidence we find you here, Ms. Weir. We tried visiting your home, but you seemed to be out?"

Felicity nodded. "I had some work."

Detective Nye nodded slowly. "Well, perhaps you

wouldn't mind answering some questions now."

"My daughter has a lot on her plate lately. She's a volunteer at the shifter camp, you know! Perhaps you could set a day and time for a more proper meeting?" Felicity's mom suggested.

Detective McMillan, who had remained silent throughout, took a sip of tea and glanced in Felicity's direction over the rim of his cup. For a moment, Felicity thought she could see a faint glow in his eyes. That wasn't possible, was it? She was under a lot of stress; perhaps she'd imagined it.

Meanwhile, Detective Nye kept staring at Felicity; he was still waiting for her answer, undeterred by what her mother had said.

"Fine. I can answer some questions. What would you like to know?"

"Why don't you take a seat, Ms. Weir." Detective Nye gestured at the empty arm chair opposite the couch. Her dad's TV chair.

Felicity held her breath as she sat down. So they had been looking for her and turned up to question her mother about her whereabouts. That wasn't a good sign. Had Alpha Squad shared their intel about her and sent the local cops after her? If, or rather, when she ran into Adam again, she would make sure to ask him.

"Well, first of all, we are the lead detectives investigating the recent string of violent crimes that had swept across Sevenoaks."

"The murders," Felicity said.

"Right. Well, livestock mutilations and indeed, the murders. We believe all of these incidents to be related."

"What would you like to know?"

"Where were you on these nights," Detective Nye asked, while handing her a sheet of paper with a list of all the dates on which the attacks had supposedly taken place. The items on the list came as no surprise to Felicity. Her anonymous tipster had called her about each of these, starting with the third or fourth animal death. This was around that time that anti-shifter sentiments had started to develop among the local population, inspiring her to start digging as well.

"Sure thing. On the third and fourth of October, I was having dinner here."

"Until what time?" Detective Nye asked.

Felicity glanced across at the other detective, who had still not uttered a single word. He had pulled out a little notepad and was waiting, pen in hand, to note Felicity's answers.

"It's been a few weeks. I don't know. I might have left around ten, maybe?"

"Both nights?" Nye asked.

Felicity nodded.

"Yes, she would have been here just until the ten o'clock news. Frank always watches the ten o'clock news right before going to bed," her mother confirmed.

"How about the other dates?" Detective Nye asked, practically ignoring her mother's input.

"Let's see." Felicity checked the list again. "On the tenth and twelfth I was at home."

"Were you alone?" Nye asked, his eyes widening just enough for Felicity to make out.

She nodded. "Yes, I live alone."

She watched helplessly as Detective Nye leaned across to his partner and half-mouthed, half-whispered the words 'no alibi.'

Unbelievable. So now her lack of social life made her a suspect? Life was so unfair.

"And you're a *shifter*, correct?" Nye asked.

Felicity gave him a blank look. He wouldn't be asking if he didn't already know. "As far as I know, that's not a crime," Felicity blurted out.

"What about yesterday. Where were you yesterday afternoon?"

Felicity started to get riled up. Who did these people think they were, anyway?

"I was at the camp. The supervisor there can confirm this; we got into an argument right around three o'clock. Plenty of people overheard."

The detectives exchanged another look.

"Well, if that's all, I hope you don't mind if I go home now," she added while getting up from her chair. This was just about all the bullshit she was willing to put up with for one day.

"We'd best be on our way as well. We might have some more questions for you later; I hope you don't mind if we get in touch again," Nye said, also getting up.

Although Felicity was reasonably tall—a side effect of her bear shifter genes—the middle aged man still had a couple of inches on her.

"Sure," she mumbled and folded her arms. No way was she shaking his hand.

Detective McMillan also got up from the sofa and Felicity caught herself staring at the man. Six foot six, at least. And a very unusual build for a human. Was he even local? It seemed unusual for a guy like this to go unnoticed in a small town like Sevenoaks. If she'd seen him in passing even once before, she might have remembered.

"Thank you, Mrs. Weir, Ms. Weir. We'll be in touch," Nye said.

Felicity nodded, but didn't say anything further. Meanwhile, her mother approached both the men, shook their hands, and thanked them for their service to the community.

On the inside, Felicity was fuming, but she did her best to keep her emotions in check. She stayed in the living room while her mother saw the two men out, and only followed into the hallway once she heard the front door click back into place.

"What the hell was that, McMillan?" Felicity heard Detective Nye's distinctive voice on the other side of the door.

Her mother was similarly frozen in place, listening.

"I wanted to observe them, focus on their body language," another voice said, probably McMillan's. That feeling that there was more to him than met the eye hit Felicity again. His voice had a certain quality to it that she could not place either. Almost familiar. But from where?

"Whatever you say, McMillan. I expect you to pull your weight going forward. I might as well have gone in there alone."

Two sets of footsteps walked away, and Felicity finally allowed herself to breathe freely.

"Thank goodness your father wasn't here to see this. Police. In our house. Looking for you!" Felicity's mom shook her head as she walked back through the hallway and into the living room.

"I haven't done anything wrong!" Felicity argued.

"What will the neighbors think?"

Felicity sighed. That was the least of her worries.

So now it wasn't just some mysterious government task force who was after her, it was the local police as well. She had to talk to Adam and figure out just what these people thought they had on her, and soon.

"Are you hungry?" her mother called out from the kitchen. "I'll make you something."

Her whole world was falling apart at the seams. How could anyone think of food at a time like this?

"No, Mom... You know what, I think I'd better go

home," Felicity said.

"Are you sure? It's no bother."

Felicity shook her head. Her work at the camp had attracted plenty of the wrong kind of attention. Now it had led the police to her parent's house. The urge to withdraw into her shell was too strong. She needed some alone time to regroup and figure out what to do next. And as much as she loved her parents, her mother's presence could be a tad distracting.

"I'm going home. I need some time by myself," she said.

Once she had said those words aloud, she realized with a heavy heart that that wasn't entirely true. There was one person—a stranger she'd only just met—whose company she craved desperately right now. Adam.

What a laugh. She had always been independent. And after just one short encounter with the man, she wanted to use him as a crutch already. It would be funny, if it wasn't so very tragic at the same time.

Alone time would do her good. With a bit of luck, she might gain some clarity by morning.

CHAPTER SEVEN

Since parting with Felicity, Adam did his best to keep his head down and follow orders. After getting back to the camp, he and Eric joined forces and questioned any bear shifters they could find. It wasn't easy. A large part of the camp's residents had come here from France and not all of them could speak English. Neither Adam nor Eric had sufficient French skills to be able to hold a meaningful conversation with these people.

So their questioning had mostly consisted of broken English and hand gestures. And one name. *Felicity*.

A lot of the residents mentioned her, mostly in passing, some extensively. It was obvious that she was a strong and well liked presence in the park. Adam did his best to ignore the skeptical looks Eric kept giving him.

By the time Alpha Squad reached the medical examiner's office, Adam felt like a whole day had passed, not just two hours or so. He was severely distracted and could not stop thinking about his short conversation with Felicity. In fact, he was so distracted that he didn't have time to worry about seeing the dead body up close and personal. An oversight that hit him as soon as the medical examiner opened the body bag.

Instantly, Adam and the rest of the team were hit by a wall of stench.

ALPHA SQUAD: FRIENDS AND FOES

So this was what death smelled like.

The sights and smells in front of him turned Adam's stomach. He tried his best to keep his breakfast down. A quick glance around the room suggested that his team mates did not appreciate the experience either. Eric and Blackwood looked more nauseous than the humans in the room. Obviously; shifter senses were much more developed.

"So as you can see, the victim, a male, in his mid-forties, was attacked viciously with a sharp, claw-like object…" The medical examiner scanned the room before proceeding. "The wounds could also suggest an attack by a large predatory animal. Defensive markings on the hands and forearms are consistent with scratch marks. Cause of death: blood loss."

Adam could not bring himself to look more closely at the body. Luckily, Bentley stepped up and partially blocked his view. "A large predatory animal, like say, a bear?" Bentley asked.

The medical examiner hesitated before continuing in a sarcastic tone. "Possibly. We don't get a lot of bear attacks here in Kent, so I don't have any previous experience…"

"I don't smell any bear," Blackwood remarked, but was quickly silenced by the disapproving looks his comment had earned him from the others in the room.

Eric cleared his throat. "Was there any evidence which could have been left behind by the attacker, any DNA?"

The medical examiner shook his head. "No, the killer was careful."

Adam frowned. The only way a shifter attack could turn out this way was if the attacker had been fully transformed. For there not to be any evidence—not even a stray bit of fur or a chipped claw—was extremely suspicious. Adam, who previously had never done much hunting, had learned as much during boot camp when all three shifters had gone into the wild together.

"I hope you don't mind if we take some pictures? Just for our records," Eric asked.

The medical examiner shrugged and stepped aside. Meanwhile, Cooper volunteered to take the pictures as the rest of them stood by and watched in silence.

Adam breathed a sigh of relief when it was all done with and the medical examiner zipped the body bag up again.

Back at the police station, the team found that yesterday's welcome committee had turned up once again, albeit in smaller numbers.

This time they had less trouble getting inside. Everyone knew exactly who they were.

Of course, that did not mean they were welcomed with open arms, far from it.

Suspicious looks and muted whispers all around as the

team found themselves waiting in the center of the incident room again, while Major Williams had a word with the chief inspector. It took a few minutes before the whole squad was ushered into another room, which was to be their temporary workspace here in Sevenoaks.

It was obvious that the room they had been given was not up for the job. Cramped was an understatement. Old file boxes and unused furniture cluttered the space. There was hardly enough room for all seven of them to sit and work; being able to move around freely inside the room was out of the question.

"Well. It is what it is," Major Williams said once she had shut the door behind them. "I'll have Callahan speak to the people at the inn to figure out if we can get some space over there. But for now, I would like everyone to report on their findings from the shifter camp."

Eric stepped up first and presented the information he had gathered with Adam. Bentley reported on the conversation Major Williams had had with the camp management.

Finally, Blackwood spoke about his inquiries among the camp's wolf population.

The longer Adam listened, the more obvious it became that a dangerous trend had developed in everyone's reports. Felicity's name was mentioned by every single one of them.

She was so active in the camp that everyone had

latched onto her as a person of interest.

"We need to find this Felicity Weir person," Major Williams concluded. "I would love to ask her a few questions."

Adam pressed his lips together and avoided Eric's intense stare. It didn't take more than a split second for the major's eyes to be fixed on Adam as well. Indeed. No secrets.

"What do we actually know about her?" Adam asked aloud. "She's a local bear shifter who helps around the camp."

"A female bear shifter. Like the one you lot sniffed out in the woods?" Bentley said. Of course the old SAS man had connected the dots.

"She was in the woods," Adam agreed.

"And you would know this, how?" Bentley asked.

"Uh…"

Adam needed to think of something quick if he didn't want this whole sordid affair to come crashing down on his head. Bentley was unpleasant enough when he *didn't* think he was being misled or lied to.

"And the medical examiner said the victim died of an apparent animal attack," Bentley remarked.

"He also said he had never seen a bear attack victim before, so how would he know for sure?" Blackwood chimed in.

Bentley scoffed.

"Guys!" Major William raised her hand. "We are

dealing with enough animosity from the locals. I will not tolerate any dissent within our own ranks. Let's keep an open mind."

Her eyes rested on Adam. "A word in private, Mr. King?"

Adam felt his heart rate increase. As soon as Eric had found out about his encounter with Felicity, this was the logical consequence. He had disobeyed a direct order.

"Yes, ma'am."

She gestured at him to follow her outside into the hallway. Luckily the local police were not using this part of the station too much, and the hallway was empty as a result.

"Speak," Major Williams said.

She knows everything, Adam told himself. *There's no point in trying to deny any of it.*

"I mean no disrespect, but I know about you and my brother," Adam started.

The look he received in response would have had lesser men quivering in their boots.

"The connection, between a shifter and his mate… It's not something that can be fought," Adam said. Was he waffling? He probably was.

"Your point being?"

She was getting impatient. This was not good.

"I am keen to make our first mission a success, and I'm determined to follow all lines of inquiry," Adam said.

"Though I feel we might be barking up the wrong tree trying to pin this on Felicity—Ms. Weir."

"If she has nothing to do with it, then our investigation will uncover as much. But as you say, we have to run down all leads. The evidence points to her as a person of interest; at the very least, she might be an important witness. And her connections in the camp make her the ideal person to talk to with regards to any threats within the refugee community."

Adam could hardly argue with that logic. "Yes, of course. We must speak to her," he grudgingly agreed.

"As a team. Not you on your own," Major Williams insisted.

"Yes, ma'am. As a team."

"Very good. Carry on, soldier." She turned on her heel and went back inside the room where the rest of the team waited.

Adam stayed outside for a minute and tried to regain his composure. No matter how good his intentions, he would not be able to shield Felicity from Alpha Squad's investigation. And if the local police got wind of them looking at her, they would want to get in on it as well. Looking at the mood in the station, as well as the angry protesters outside, there was little hope of *them* being open minded and leaving their prejudices aside when speaking to her. They would be quick to point fingers, just like Bentley had done.

When Adam finally went back into the room, he found

his brother staring at him already. This *no secrets* business was quite difficult to deal with. After living a largely independent life, Adam had never appreciated family or any authority figure looking at his choices with so much scrutiny. Alpha Squad training might be over, but he still had a lot to get used to.

"Guys, check this out," Cooper spoke up, much to everyone's surprise. The younger and least experienced human on the team had had little to contribute to the investigation so far.

Adam, as well as the rest of the team, gathered around Cooper, who held up his phone.

He pressed play on a video.

"Rachel Kinsey reporting for Sky News, here with an exclusive from Sevenoaks, Kent, where a recent string of violent attacks has left a number of livestock and three people dead so far. Protesters are gathering around the town center to voice their dissent over the government's decision of situating a shifter refugee camp here just on the outskirts of the city…"

So far, old news.

But then the camera panned off to the right, where a middle aged man stood on a small podium in front of the local supermarket they had passed by this morning on the way to the camp.

"Welcome, fellow men and women. I am Victor Domnall, and I'm here to tell you—you are not alone in your struggle."

"Oh, shit," Blackwood blurted out.

Adam's entire body tensed up at the sight of the man. Although his organization, the Sons of Domnall, had been the shifters' mortal enemy for many generations, their illustrious leader had only popped up in the spotlight shortly after Eric and the rest of the New Alliance had orchestrated the exposure of shifterkind in the media earlier in the year.

A classic opportunist.

Now that the human population knew about shifters, he was trying to cash in on any fear and prejudice that lingered. It was no real surprise that he'd turned up here in Sevenoaks to make the most of the crime spree they had come in to investigate.

Still, that didn't pacify Adam much. Wherever Victor Domnall went, the national and sometimes international media followed. His presence here meant much more public scrutiny. The pressure was on. The local police would be in a rush to find the killer.

And if Adam had learned anything from every crime drama or TV series he'd ever watched: public pressure rarely resulted in the right decisions being made.

Alpha Squad only had one person of interest so far, Felicity.

ALPHA SQUAD: FRIENDS AND FOES

Although Major Williams had done her best to remind him of his responsibilities to the squad, he knew that if he was made to choose, his loyalties would lie firmly with Felicity.

CHAPTER EIGHT

It was still dark out when Felicity was rudely awoken by her phone ringing off the hook. Her instincts kicked in instantly and she jerked upright, knocking over the lamp on her bedside table in order to get to the phone.

"Hello? Who is it?" she answered. In her rush, she hadn't even bothered to check the caller ID.

"Felicity!" a panicked female voice called out to her. "Fire! There's fire, everywhere!"

Felicity recognized the voice as one of the women she'd been working with at the camp, Sophie. She was a single mother of two, and the one person with the best command of the English language out of the whole lot.

Felicity jumped out of bed and checked the time on her alarm clock. Just after six.

"What fire? What's going on?"

"I don't know, but Felicity, please come quickly. We are under attack!"

The line went dead, leaving Felicity with more questions than answers. A fire at the camp. So many families living so closely together… This could turn into a catastrophe.

She did her best to get dressed using only one hand while using the other to dial emergency services.

"Hello? I want to report a fire at the shifter camp,"

ALPHA SQUAD: FRIENDS AND FOES

Felicity said as soon as someone answered on the other end.

"Please state your name."

"Felicity Weir. Please hurry, there are families there. Children."

"Thank you, Ms. Weir. We are aware of the situation."

Fine. That was all she needed to know.

Felicity did not waste time with any niceties, she just cut the call and finished getting dressed as quickly as she possibly could.

It was only a matter of time. Ever since the protests started, she had worried about things escalating. Victor Domnall's press conference in town, which she'd had the misfortune of catching on TV the previous night, should have tipped her off that the tide was closing in.

After weeks of uncertainty and finger-pointing, some fanatic had taken matters into their own hands and attacked the camp.

She gathered her coat and keys and ran out of the house, straight to her car. Of course, she wasn't a firefighter. She couldn't help, at least directly, but this was personal. Someone had attacked *her* people, and nothing and no one could keep Felicity away.

***

It was six-fifteen when Adam's sleep was interrupted by loud banging on the door to the room he shared with Blackwood.

"Huh, what?" the wolf called out as he sat up straight in his bed.

It took Adam a few seconds more to acknowledge the intrusion.

"What's going on?" he called out.

"Get up. We push out in five," Eric's voice shouted through the door.

Adam rubbed his eyes and forced himself out of bed. It wasn't so much that he minded the early start. It was the unexpected timing of it that frazzled him.

Something must have happened. Something bad.

He threw on his uniform as quickly as he could and grudgingly shared the space around the small sink with Blackwood to brush his teeth. Within minutes, the two shifters were ready.

Footsteps could already be heard moving out of the hallway outside their room. Alpha Squad was nothing if not efficient.

They joined the rest of the team outside in the Inn's parking lot, where Major Williams was busy making a phone call. Eric waited by her side with his hands folded.

"Yes, Mr. Teese. I understand that the Ministry of Shifter Affairs wants Alpha Squad to take a leading role in this, but we are dealing with influences outside our control here. Yes, Sir. I will report back to your office as soon as I have any information of note. Suspects? It's really too early to tell. We are following all leads. Yes, absolutely."

The major's expression was tense when she hung up.

"Get into the Land Rover. We are heading to the camp," she said.

Adam raised his eyebrows and shot Eric a curious look. *What was going on? Had they found another body?*

Of course, Eric couldn't hear his question; that would be weird. And anyway, his brother was much more focused on Major Williams than on Adam. *Obviously.*

As soon as they found themselves in the back of the Land Rover, Adam voiced his question aloud.

"So, what's going down at the camp?" Adam asked.

The others lifted their heads and stared first at Adam, then at Eric, whom the question was directed at.

"They've been attacked."

Blackwood inhaled sharply.

Bentley shrugged. "That's not a surprise." He could be such an ass.

"Are they okay?" Adam asked, ignoring Bentley's comment on purpose.

Eric leaned forward and looked out the window. "Apparently someone's set a fire, but it's too early to say tell what exactly the situation is on ground. That's why we're heading in. Those shifters in the camp fall under our purview as well."

"I see," Adam mumbled. He sat back and tried to remain calm. This was terrible news. It was so early still that hopefully Felicity wouldn't have been at the camp when things went bad, but until they got there, he couldn't be sure of that either.

Hopefully she was okay. Hopefully they all were.

Adam remained quietly lost in his own web of worries and concerns for the remainder of the drive.

Finally, they pulled into the driveway of the camp, where they came to a halt.

"Alpha Squad, open the gate!" Major Williams could be heard clearly in the back of the Land Rover.

"Ma'am, it would be best, if…" a voice stammered.

"Step aside, soldier!" she barked. "We are under authority of the Secretary of Shifter Affairs, just as you are. If you value your job, you will let us in right this moment!"

Adam did not have that much patience. He climbed over Blackwood, who was blocking his exit, and jumped out of the back of the vehicle. He was already sprinting up the drive toward the camp, when the Land Rover started moving again behind him.

"Adam!" he heard Eric call out for him.

Adam did not look back though and continued to run. His eyes were focused solely on the orange glow ahead. The smell of charred wood stung against the inside of his nose. He thought he could even feel the heat already, though he was still some distance away from the actual fire.

That was when he felt *her*. Felicity was here somewhere and his heart started to beat even faster.

She was his first priority. Making sure she was safe. Only then would he be able to focus on anything else, including his actual purpose here, to represent Alpha Squad.

Felicity! His inner bear was raging inside his chest, and he wasn't the only one losing control.

As Adam ran past the first house, he saw what could have very well been a young version of himself: a teenage boy, mid-shift, his expression a mix of fear and determination as he ran away from the carnage. Everyone's instincts were in overdrive. That was what happened when a shifter felt threatened or cornered; his animal side clawed its way to the surface in order to deal.

Adam stopped in front of the administrative building; this was where the management had their offices, only now it was engulfed by flames. He could feel her more keenly now. Felicity was inside. Right in the heart of it all.

Adam broke past some guards who tried to block his access, but they were no match for him.

"Felicity!" he called out as he entered the smoke-filled building.

There was no answer. He knew he was getting closer though, running through the corridor toward the back of the building where the fire seemed to have started.

The heat was intense.

He could feel her. He thought he could even hear the thump of her heartbeat. His own seemed to beat in sync with hers.

"Felicity!" he shouted again.

"In here," she responded. "Help me!"

He burst through the door separating them, and saw that she was surrounded by flames.

In her arms, she cradled a young child, a girl who couldn't have been more than four years old.

"She's not moving!" Felicity screamed.

With every passing moment, the smoke inside what looked like a classroom was getting denser and more pungent. It was hard to breathe already. The longer they stayed here, the more danger they were in.

Adam took a few seconds to scan the room. It wouldn't be long before the structure of the building would give way. Or a window would burst open and let in more oxygen, causing the fire to swell even further. They were out of time.

Adam didn't think any further; he let his bear take over and ran straight through the fire to reach Felicity.

He carried her as well as the child back the way he came. Flames licked at his fur, but he didn't feel a thing. All he could think of was her. To get her out of here before she was seriously hurt.

Within thirty seconds or so, Adam had found his way back through the maze he'd navigated to get here and they could all breathe somewhat fresher air again.

He didn't care that the human staff of the camp was staring at him. He barely even noticed the rest of Alpha Squad as he passed them by on the way to the ambulance.

"Please, take care of her," he said to the terrified

paramedic. The latter did nothing but stare. He didn't even move a muscle or make any attempt to help.

What the hell! Do something already! he thought.

You're shifted, another voice spoke in his mind.

He looked down to find Felicity looking up at him. He could hear her, finally.

And she was right, of course.

He set Felicity and the girl down in front of the paramedic and withdrew. Shifters weren't generally shy about their bodies, but he thought it wise to get out of view first before transforming back into his human self. There were a lot of people about this morning, who might not understand or appreciate the sight of his transformation.

So he ran into the woods where Felicity and he had first spoken. There, he forced the animal back inside. It was cold this morning. He hadn't noticed until just now. Looking down at himself, he couldn't help but wonder how he might get out of here without attracting even more attention.

The answer to his problem presented itself in the form of Eric, who came running in his direction.

"Adam, what the hell do you think you're doing?" he demanded.

"Look, she was in trouble. What was I supposed to do, let her die in there?" Adam straightened himself, placed his hands on his hips, and stared his brother down. His move was clear; any shifter would have recognized it as a classic leadership challenge.

Eric backed off, though his dark expression made it obvious that his reaction did not come from a position of submission.

"Had it been the major in there, what would you have done?" Adam pointed out, as he let his shoulders slump a little. The challenge was over. He had won, for now.

"Fine. Okay. But we have a job to do here. An image and a reputation to protect. Everyone already treats us like we're some joke, and you strutting around the place full-bear is not helping in any way!"

"It was the only way I could get through the fire, bro."

"There are going to be consequences," Eric said. His tone was flat. It not a threat, just a statement of fact. "I can't shield you from the fallout, little brother."

"I know and I'll take responsibility for it all. But first, I'm going to need a new uniform or something," Adam said.

Eric nodded and marched back in the direction he came from, passing Felicity on the way. They exchanged a strange look—part understanding, part apprehension—but Eric kept on walking, thankfully.

You're okay, Adam thought. The sight of her, zig-zagging through the trees in order to reach him, made him smile.

You're not so bad yourself, she responded.

He glanced down at himself and shrugged sheepishly. *It*

comes with the territory.

She stopped just a couple of feet away. His inner bear wasn't ready to accept that, so Adam bridged the gap himself.

Guided purely by instinct, he leaned down, cupped her face in his hand, and planted his lips on top of hers. She did not resist. They both wanted this; he could feel it. He'd been so scared of her getting hurt in the fire; his relief was equally intense.

Her taste, so sweet, was like nectar straight from the most fragrant of flowers.

Her soft lips could have made a lesser man cry, they felt so delicate.

He could just about see a glimpse of the glow in her eyes before she shut them involuntarily, as he shut his.

A warmth filled Adam which he had never felt before. Like he was home. He belonged.

"Wait a moment." Eric's voice disrupted their moment of perfection.

"Step aside," another vaguely familiar voice demanded. It was the older one of the two unpleasant detectives who had briefed the squad at the police station.

Adam let go of Felicity and opened his eyes. The man was just fifteen feet away, looking right at him and Felicity with a smug grin on his face.

"Well, this is certainly a surprise," he said, making it a point to stare down at Adam's naked form.

Oh God, kill me now. Adam sighed.

I hate this guy, Felicity agreed.

Those consequences Eric had warned him of were about to come crashing down on him and possibly her as well. Nobody, not even Alpha Squad, would be able to get him out of this one.

CHAPTER NINE

Never before had Felicity believed that she needed anyone; not really. She had always handled her life, both professional and personal, on her own. Sure, she sometimes confided in her parents. In the past, she'd at times confided in her ex-best friend, Joy, but none of those interactions had made her feel anything like what she felt now with Adam.

The memory of their kiss was still fresh. She could still feel a tingle in the exact spot where his lips had touched hers. Their connection was intense. Not just because it was new, but because it was real. She'd felt *the bond*. She'd heard his thoughts and felt his feelings and felt at one with him.

It had come to an end much too soon.

"Ms. Weir, if you don't mind… I asked you a question!" Detective Nye insisted.

She shook her head and tried to focus. What question?

"I'm sorry?" she stammered.

"Why were you at the camp this morning?" the detective repeated himself.

Felicity frowned at him. Was he serious?

"For the same reason you were, I imagine?"

"I want to hear it in your own words," the man said.

She shook her head in disbelief. Was he being thick on purpose or what?

"I got a call about the fire, and I came as soon as I could. One of the families I work with, their youngest was stuck inside one of the classrooms. I did my best to get her out."

"The child is what, a wolf? Some other animal?" the detective asked.

Felicity was getting more and more frustrated. What sort of questions were these? "If you must know, shifters don't acquire the ability to transform until puberty. So technically she would be no different from any *human* child."

"And then?"

And then... The fire had blocked her exit; she feared certain death, but then Adam had arrived. Surely people would have seen all that? Why on earth ask all these daft questions?

"Adam got us out of the building."

"U-huh, Adam, you say. Adam King, member of Alpha Squad and bear shifter, just like you are, correct?"

"I suppose so," Felicity mumbled.

"Right." Detective Nye went quiet as he made some notes, presumably of her answers.

Felicity tried to compose herself, but instead, her anger flared up. How dare this guy waste her time as though she had done something wrong? And Adam, as well. He had saved them. Who the hell did this idiot think he was?

"Can I go now?" she said. "I'm assuming I'm not under arrest for trying to save an innocent four-year-old, right?"

ALPHA SQUAD: FRIENDS AND FOES

Detective Nye smiled briefly, though it was obviously disingenuous. His eyes were too cold and calculating, making his attempt at a smile look more like a grimace.

"Good," Felicity said and walked off without acknowledging the man any further. She wasn't quite sure what his deal was, but he really had it in for her. The way he'd even attempted to twist the rescue of a young child from a fire into something negative. Obviously, this man had issues and prejudices against her kind that severely impaired his judgment.

And now that he had questioned her on his own, without his partner being present, all that ugliness had come out to the forefront.

As she made her way through the park to the group of refugees that was huddled together at a safe distance, Felicity wondered idly where Detective Nye's rather quiet partner had gone. She still felt there was something strange about that guy, though she couldn't quite work out what it was.

She shook off all these thoughts by the time she reached the families she had come to know during the last few weeks.

"Good, you're all safe," Felicity said, with as genuine a smile on her lips as she could muster.

"Oh, Felicity! It was terrible!" Sophie walked up to her and gave her a big hug.

"It still looks that way. How did it start?" Felicity asked.

"I tried to tell the policeman, but I don't think he was really listening," Sophie complained; her accent seemed heavier now that she was upset. She took a deep breath and rested her hand on her son's shoulder. He stood beside her with his own arms wrapped around his little sister. The fear in their eyes was heartbreaking.

"I woke up hearing what I thought were footsteps. Two, maybe three men, but only one of them spoke like he was giving orders. I don't know how, but I could feel danger. I woke up the children and started calling out for everyone. Then I heard the glass. The windows on the common building."

"And then?" Felicity urged.

"Well then, the fire started, it looked like it started everywhere at the same time. Most of us were already awake. The big building was on fire, and people were running in a panic."

"Did you see the men who did it?"

"*Non*. They must have left when they noticed us leaving our houses."

"And you didn't recognize the voice of the man in charge?" Felicity asked.

Sophie shook her head, her eyes moist and heavy. This morning's ordeal had taken its toll on everyone.

Felicity wrapped her arms around Sophie's shoulder again.

"I'll do what I can to find the people who did this. They will not get away with it," Felicity said. It was a risky promise to make, especially with the local police breathing down her neck. But she had to. She owed it to these people to find out who wanted to harm them.

She wasn't even sure how and where to start. Ever since the horrific attacks on the local population, it seemed like every human in Sevenoaks was out to get the shifter refugees, and that was before Victor Domnall brought his media circus to town. Finding out exactly who was involved in this arson attack would be a very tall order indeed.

At least she wouldn't be doing it on her own. She'd ask Adam to help; perhaps with his special Alpha Squad training and access, he could fill in the blanks and find out everything she couldn't.

Adam could do nothing but watch as Detective Nye led Felicity away. Thankfully, Eric had got him a random spare uniform from the Land Rover, which he'd put on in a rush. It was small, but better than nothing.

His own uniform would be burnt to a crisp along with the rest of the building by now. He could still hear the crackle of the raging fire, even though he was quite a distance away from it, shielded by the trees. Evidently the fire department felt it was best to wait and let the flames die down on their own.

"This isn't good," Eric remarked, as he continued to

stare in the direction the detective had left in with Felicity. "Janine—the major wants to talk to you."

Eric and Adam shared a quick look. He might not like it, but Eric understood. Adam could see as much in his eyes. He would have done the same thing for Major Williams, even if he hadn't admitted it aloud earlier.

"Well then, time to face the music," Adam grumbled as he followed Eric out of the woods.

On his way across the now largely abandoned camp, he caught a glimpse of Felicity, who was being questioned by the unpleasant detective. Oh, how he longed to rip that man's face right off. His entire presence, from his ugly face to his threatening body language, rubbed Adam the wrong way.

And worse still, he could *feel* the tension she felt. The frustration, the anger at being cornered once again by this guy. He wanted to protect her, keep her from all this unpleasantness, but intervening now would just make things worse for both of them.

"Quit staring," Eric hissed at him and led him on further to the Alpha Squad vehicle.

"There you are," Major Williams started.

Adam kept his eyes fixed on the ground ahead of him. It was all he could do to stop himself from turning back and telling that idiot detective to stop harassing his woman.

"Let's go, guys. I'm sure they can still use our help around here," Eric said, ushering the rest of the team away from the vehicle.

Bentley and Cooper gave Adam some odd looks as they walked off. Perhaps it was one of their uniforms that Eric had found, explaining the size difference. Or perhaps the sight of him fully transformed had shocked them.

Major Williams cleared her throat as soon as the others were out of earshot.

"I realize there's a learning curve here, Mr. King."

Adam wasn't sure what to make of her tone. Was it frustration, exasperation?

"You came to the squad with a rather difficult history," she added.

Adam glanced down at the floor. She disapproved of his actions, obviously. Could they skip past the lecture already and find some kind of solution for what happened at the camp, though? This was just a waste of time.

"Ma'am, no disrespect, but I did save two lives this morning," Adam said.

The major pressed her lips together and kept her eyes firmly locked onto his. She did not appreciate being interrupted.

"That's true, and commendable. But I implore you to understand that context means nothing here. You went in and saved lives. You know this; I know this; the people involved know this. Unfortunately, you also came out of that building in bear form, which to a large part of the population would be a rather terrifying image."

Adam shook his head. So this was about image now?

"What happened to doing good work? To making a difference?"

The major sighed. "Look, you had your orders. You weren't going to go off on your own anymore. We could have gone in as a team—"

Adam glanced up at the major's stern expression. She was Eric's mate. That basically made her his sister-in-law as well as his boss. It was awkward and inconvenient, and Eric would disapprove, but nobody could keep him from going in and saving Felicity.

Not even the major and her orders.

If he'd waited for the rest of the team, who knew what could have happened? They might not have even made it into the building on time.

"I touched upon this when you pulled me aside last time, Ma'am. I know about you and Eric. And I'm not just saying that, or trying to use that information to apply any kind of pressure. I *know*. I feel the same way about Felicity. I cannot fight it, neither do I want to."

"It's up to you then, soldier. We are here to do a job. And if we fail, it doesn't just affect the people in this town, it could affect the future of the squad. I cannot have loose cannons on the team."

Was she trying to say what he thought she was? Was this an ultimatum?

"We've discussed this during boot camp. You know where I stand. I want Alpha Squad to succeed just like the rest of the guys. But I cannot turn my back on my mate. I just physically cannot do it."

Adam stared at the major, and she stared back. He wasn't being as overtly rebellious as earlier with his brother, but she had challenged him, and his instincts had responded in kind.

"Then I suggest you sit this one out. As it is, I'll have the locals breathing down my neck now about our involvement with Felicity Weir. If they find out about the evidence we gathered that night at the crime scene, and put two and two together that you're a couple, everything we've worked for will fall apart."

Adam nodded. As much as it pained him, there was no other choice.

"As you wish, Major Williams."

He turned on his heel and marched off, still painfully aware that the spare uniform Eric had given him wasn't exactly his size and pinched awkwardly in all the wrong places.

"I'll still want to question her! As soon as we're done with the clean-up here," the major called after him.

Whatever happened next, Felicity and he were on their own. But that was okay; he already knew what his first move should be. To hell with *police procedures 101* and other rules. All bets were off now.

From the corner of his eye, Adam saw that Detective Nye was alone again. Evidently, he had finished harassing

Felicity. He changed direction just enough to ensure that their paths would cross, then accidentally—on purpose—bumped into the detective.

"Excuse me," Adam mumbled.

It was such a stereotypical move the entire situation might have been comical, if the stakes weren't so high.

"Watch where you're going!" Nye complained, rubbing his shoulder.

Adam faked a smile, secure in the knowledge that his stunt had paid off. Within the blink of an eye, he had located the detective's notebook and stowed it away safely in a pocket of his too-small tactical vest.

Who knew that those couple of years spent in what his folks had called 'the wrong company' would pay off now. Pickpocketing turned out to be a rather useful skill, after all.

"And, Mr. King, I'm going to want to talk to you before the day is over!" Detective Nye called after him.

Adam rolled his eyes. Not likely. "You can discuss that with my squad leader," Adam responded.

CHAPTER TEN

After her run-in with Detective Nye, Felicity had stayed at the camp for a few more hours, just to make sure that the families she had worked with all these weeks were somewhat settled.

The administrative building had been the worst affected, but some of the residential units had also been damaged in the fire. The ones that were still standing were now doubly occupied as most families had taken in some of the now homeless refugees.

And that wasn't even the worst thing; these families had left their homes following increasing hostilities aimed at them simply for who they were. They had tried to flee from this same kind of danger in their home countries, and now the place they had run to for safety had betrayed them.

It had been a big shock for everyone. Felicity's heart hurt for everyone affected. At the same time, she was overwhelmed by a deep, stinging shame. It was *her* town that had turned on them. The people she had grown up with were responsible. And if given half a chance, they wouldn't care that she was a local, born and bred in Sevenoaks. They would turn on her too.

The mood had not just soured; it was rotten and beyond saving. That was how it felt, anyway.

She was in a good mood to run and never look back, if it wasn't for all these people depending on her.

When she started looking into the attacks herself, she had felt like the investigation was the answer to everyone's problems. If only she could prove that the shifters had nothing to do with the murders, the hostilities would die down. Now she wasn't so sure anymore.

Tensions had risen to dangerous levels. And as her interactions with Detective Nye had already proved, it was extremely difficult to argue with zealots who had already made up their minds about everything. The sort of people who would take it upon themselves to attack a camp full of vulnerable families with small children, would they really back down, ever? Even if the murder case was resolved, and it was clearly proven that the shifters had nothing to do with it all, would it really make any difference?

Was there any hope left for these people? For this town?

It was almost noon by the time Felicity took a breather and sat down on one of the tree stumps that lined the edge of the camp. The clean-up was well underway, thanks to the people from Alpha Squad, though strangely, Adam was nowhere to be found since their encounter in the woods. Perhaps that was for the best. She might not have been able to focus on anything else if he was around.

The refugees were now settled for the most part.

And Felicity was beat, both physically and emotionally.

"Felicity, thank you so much for everything," a familiar

voice spoke.

She looked up to find Sophie standing beside her. The woman looked beat herself.

"It's no problem," Felicity mumbled.

"Why don't you go home, rest a bit? We'll manage things here," Sophie said.

Although she didn't want to admit it, Felicity knew that Sophie was right. She ought to head home, maybe lie down for a bit. Like this she was no help to anyone.

"Fine. But promise you'll call me if anything else happens," Felicity said, as she forced herself back onto her feet.

"Of course. It will be okay. *We* will be okay, I can feel it," Sophie said.

Felicity studied the woman's face for a few seconds. She couldn't be sure if she was being honest, or just saying what she thought Felicity needed to hear to keep it together.

"The people from Alpha Squad are going to stay and make sure the camp is secure," Felicity mumbled.

Sophie nodded. "I know. They told me."

"Okay then, I will see you tomorrow," Felicity said.

Sophie stepped up and gave her a warm hug. Only then did Felicity notice just how sore she was. Her shoulders, her back, even her arms were aching. She forced a smile, and tried not to let it show.

"Bye, Felicity," Sophie said.

Felicity nodded and headed to her car, pausing before turning the key in the ignition. Where *was* Adam, actually? She hadn't seen him in hours. Perhaps they'd sent him off to do something else while the rest of the squad helped at the camp.

Although his absence was a bit odd, Felicity knew deep in her heart that she'd see him again soon. That thought alone kept her going as she drove back home.

Felicity wasn't sure what woke her up. It wasn't a noise, but a sensation or a presence. She blinked a few times and stared at the ceiling.

There it was again.

A tug in her chest which told her she wasn't alone.

It wasn't a bad feeling; it was reassuring and warm, like a cozy blanket to keep the cold out. A smile formed on her lips. It was Adam.

Felicity got up and made her way through the living room straight to the front door.

There he was.

"Hi," she said, and opened the door wide.

"I didn't disturb you, did I?" he asked.

She shook her head. "You came just at the right time."

Felicity stepped aside and watched him enter. There was something different about him now. He was a mess of feelings and thoughts, making it hard for Felicity to focus on any one of them.

"What's going on?" she asked. *How did you know where I live?* Of course, she didn't mind him turning up here, but that didn't make her less curious.

Adam turned and fiddled with his vest, retrieving a familiar looking notepad and holding it up in her direction.

"I got this off the detective," Adam said in a matter-of-fact tone.

Felicity took the notepad and studied it carefully. A rare glimpse into the inner workings of the mind of her main enemy on the police force. "You stole this?" she said. She wasn't even sure she wanted to know the exact circumstances under which he obtained it.

Adam shrugged. "Borrowed it. I was hoping to get insight into the police investigation. They're not exactly telling us anything."

Felicity frowned. "No? I thought Alpha Squad was collaborating with the police."

"Yeah, we thought so too. It's a rather one-sided affair."

If that was the case, then why was he here sharing the detective's notes with her and not with his team mates…?

There's something you're not telling me.

Adam pressed his lips together. *I'm sorry.*

Felicity stepped up to him and rested her hand on his arm. *What is it?*

"I'm off the team. At least for now. The major wants to

avoid any appearance of impropriety."

Felicity sank down onto the sofa, her hands tightening around the notepad. *Now what?*

Adam sat down next to her and took her hand. A jolt of electricity passed from his skin into hers; at least that was the nearest description to how it felt.

I'm so sorry. But no matter what, we'll figure things out together.

Felicity closed her eyes and tried to think. But all that achieved was to flood her mind with imagery of their kiss in the woods. How did shifter couples achieve anything at all, when the intense attraction between them overwhelmed everything else, even rational thought?

"It'll be okay, right?" Felicity mumbled.

"I know it will." Adam wrapped his arm around her and held her close.

She could hear his heartbeat so clearly. How it had sped up the moment they touched and continued to hammer away at a feverish pace now that she was safely tucked in his embrace. Perhaps this was the right thing to do. Perhaps they owed it to themselves as well as each other to blow off some steam, so that they could dive into the investigation with renewed vigor and focus.

That was her justification to satisfy her mind anyway. Her heart and body didn't care to rationalize; they just wanted to act.

Adam sensed the change in her; of course he did. Such was their connection.

He scooped her up off the couch and carried her

through the short hallway into the bedroom. It was a mess; the bed wasn't made and laundry was piled up on the chair that stood by the wardrobe. Felicity might have felt awkward about the state of the room with anyone else, but not with Adam. He hadn't even noticed it.

His eyes were fixed on hers.

His hands roamed her body, unbuttoning, undressing, peeling away the layers until she lay naked before him.

The entire scene happened in a haze of passion. Felicity didn't consciously *do* anything; neither did Adam, probably. Things just... happened.

Clothes, discarded on the floor.

Limbs entwined in ecstasy.

Sheets crumpled underneath her back.

They kissed until their lips were sore, nibbled and licked at any body part that came within reach.

Their fingertips explored every curve and crevice.

The air was heavy with the scent of arousal.

Their heads filled with images of pleasure.

This was the endgame, the supreme purpose of their connection. This was what their bodies, hearts, and minds had worked toward since their first meeting.

Propriety and morality didn't hold any relevance. Biology dictated that this was what they do: celebrate their union. Please each other. Allow their spirits to merge into one.

Adam spread Felicity's legs and dove down, licking her

most intimate parts. Making her cry out with the intensity of it all.

She lifted herself onto her elbows and looked down at him. His face diving down again and again, teasing, tempting, seducing…

It was the most beautiful sight; the way he looked up at her from between her thighs.

But lying helplessly on her back wasn't natural for her. She struggled to regain control and turn the tables.

Adam allowed it, barely.

She went down on him, teasing him with her tongue until he hit the brink of pleasure, causing him to push her away.

Not like this.

Felicity got up on all fours and circled him, as he did the same, with the mattress wobbling awkwardly underneath them. To an outside observer, it would have looked more like the start of a nude wrestling match than lovemaking.

It was a game, in a way. A competition to see who would push the other over the finish line first.

Finally, they came together again. Adam wrapped his arms around her waist, lifting her on top of his lap. This was a suitable compromise; they were both somewhat in control.

It didn't take them long to find their rhythm.

She rode him, guided by his hands on her hips, faster and harder.

ALPHA SQUAD: FRIENDS AND FOES

Although she wanted it to, the moment didn't last. They were too far gone, too hormonal and impatient.

When Felicity's orgasm hit, she could feel a similar surge of pleasure pass through him. They were perfectly timed, perfectly matched.

Perfectly mated.

Adam continued to hold on to her. His powerful arms cradled her as they both caught their breath. This was how they stayed for a while longer, neither willing to move or change anything at all.

Finally, Felicity's heart rate settled, as did her breathing.

She closed her eyes and nuzzled Adam's neck. This was her new safe place. Her sanctuary.

With Adam's arms still wrapped around her, slowly, Felicity's faculties started to return. The calmer her body became, the faster her mind tried to work. It had just been an excuse, but now that they'd released the tension between them, she did find room in her mind for other thoughts. At last, they'd achieved clarity.

"This is just part of the picture, that horrible detective's note pad," she said, breaking the silence.

If they weren't already in each other's thoughts, her comment would have been weirdly out of context. Luckily, he was right here with her, thinking the same thoughts.

Adam leaned back slightly and glanced up at her. "What are you saying?"

"Well, seeing as we don't have any outside help

anymore, it's more important than ever to figure out what we're up against. You know Alpha Squad doesn't have any viable leads, but neither do they have access to everything the police has. How will they ever solve the case without all the facts? How will we?"

A smile crept over Adam's face. "I see where you're going with this. It'll be dark soon; that's when we'll get our chance."

Felicity didn't dare say anything else. Was she asking too much? He was already risking his career for her; if they went any further, his freedom might be at stake as well.

Anything for you, Adam's thoughts reassured her. *Don't worry.*

She still felt bad for having the idea, but the sad fact was, this was the only way they'd find out the whole truth. There was simply no other way of moving the investigation forward.

It was the two of them against the world.

CHAPTER ELEVEN

———◆———

It was after ten o'clock when Adam and Felicity pulled up into a parking space a couple of blocks away from the police station. The town was quiet; the shops had closed hours ago. The only place that still showed signs of activity was a pub, halfway down the road from the station.

Years had passed since Adam's trouble-making younger days, but he felt ready. If they were going to solve the case, it simply had to be done.

Felicity looked nervous, how she was gripping the steering wheel so tightly with both her hands; it was endearing.

Don't worry, I know what I'm doing, Adam tried to reassure her.

She forced a smile. *I just don't want you to get into trouble.*

I won't. Trust me.

He leaned across and kissed her on the cheek. The change in her was instant; she took a deep breath and visibly relaxed.

"I'm so glad we're in this together now," she whispered.

Me too.

Adam scanned their surroundings. Unlike his old hunting grounds in East London, this place was so much quieter. That was a double-edged sword; he was less likely to be seen by random passers-by, but at the same time, if someone did spot him, it would rouse more suspicion. He had to rely on every one of his super-human talents, as well as certain learned skills, to pull this off.

Adam nodded at Felicity, his mate, the woman he'd never realized he was waiting for all his life, and exited the vehicle.

This was all for her.

He bridged the gap between Felicity's car and the police station in record time, sprinting around the back of the building and looking for the most sensible way in. There were some surveillance cameras, but they were spaced wide enough apart that he remained unseen by any of them as he located the power mains that fed the security system.

He wasn't a master criminal, far from it, so it was sheer luck that the system employed by the local police was sub-par and very easy to disable. It didn't even seem to have a phone connection to alert anyone of a breach, just a siren, which Adam managed to disconnect without issue.

Once he had identified the most logical way in, a ventilator window most likely belonging to the station's restrooms, Adam disabled the nearest camera with a well-aimed throw of a rock he found lying around on the ground. He used his Alpha Squad issue tactical knife to wedge the window out of its frame and carefully place it against the base of the wall.

Within the blink of an eye, he was inside.

Adam wasted no time; he headed straight for the

conference room where the squad had been briefed on their first day and systematically took pictures of all the material he found pinned to the wall. Then he moved on to the workstations in the common area of the station. It took him a minute or two to identify Detective Nye's desk, which housed a big stack of dossiers relating to the various attacks.

It was a lot of material, written in small type, so there was little hope of it being photographed clearly in the dark, so he picked up everything and was about to leave, when he saw the copier in the corner. Best not to tip the police off to his presence here…

He waited impatiently for the copy machine to work its way through all the pages he deemed relevant. Funny, how such a normal sound could be so deafeningly loud when you were breaking and entering… Then, he stuffed the copies into a blank file he found, and put the originals back just how he had found them in Detective Nye's desk.

Within minutes, he backtracked his way to the window he'd entered from, climbed out of the building, and did his best to push the glass panel back into place.

With a bit of luck, they'd assume their broken camera had just failed on its own and nobody would be the wiser once they came in the next morning.

On the drive home, Felicity could feel the adrenaline coursing through her veins. Maybe this was somewhat how Bonnie and Clyde had felt, like outlaws, whose criminal actions had somehow felt justified as well.

Before teaming up with Adam, wandering around a cordoned off crime scene at night had been the worst she'd ever done. Now she was an accessory in a break-in. One might say Adam was a bad influence, only it had been Felicity's idea to break into the police station in the first place.

Still, it was all for a good cause.

Now that they were back at Felicity's place, she felt more positive than ever. With the official files from the police station, Detective Nye's notes as well as the evidence both Adam and Felicity had found at the final crime scene, they would be so close to putting the puzzle that was the string of gruesome murders together.

Everything was falling into place, and it was just a matter of time before they'd succeed.

What a new feeling. What a relief. And it was all thanks to Adam.

She let herself fall back into the sofa and watched as Adam took off his coat. He was a beautiful man, with or without clothes on. Even that little crease between his eyebrows that appeared when he was really deep in thought did not detract. If anything, it was endearing.

He opened the big dossier files he'd taken from the station and sat down next to her.

"It's all got to be here. All the answers. I'm sure of it. We just have to put it together just right," he said.

Felicity smiled. She felt the same way. But now that they had joined forces, she felt a lot less pressure.

"What do you say we give it a rest, just for the rest of the night?" Felicity suggested, and fished the file out of Adam's hands, closed it, and placed it on the coffee table in front of them.

Adam glanced at her and smiled subtly. "What do you have in mind?"

Of course *that was* where his mind had gone. Again. She couldn't blame him; in fact, she felt the same. But there was something else she wanted from him first.

"In time," Felicity said. "First, I want to know you. Not just little glimpses or details. I want to know who you are, really. I can tell there's something on your mind that you're not telling me."

Adam didn't answer straight away. The crease on his forehead deepened.

"One of the guys on the team is my older brother," Adam began.

Felicity leaned against him, and sighed deeply when Adam lifted his arm and wrapped it around her. "Of course. The resemblance is striking."

He ran his fingertip up and down on her upper arm. It made her tickle, in more ways than one.

Felicity closed her eyes and tried to really listen.

"He's always looked out for me, even when I did my best to push him away. I'm sure he's pretty unhappy about me getting kicked off the squad."

Felicity turned and looked up at him. As an only child, she couldn't imagine how he must feel.

"You think you let him down?" she asked.

Adam shrugged. "I dunno. I mean, we don't *talk*. Not like you and I are doing now."

"Well, obviously. We're mates. You're brothers. It's different."

He nodded. "Yeah, it is different, isn't it? And the thing is, he ought to understand what happened here. He found his mate not so long ago. He should know how it feels to be torn between professional responsibilities and this… This deeper, more intimate thing."

Felicity pressed her lips together. She felt for him. He'd lost his position in the squad over her. And helping her with this investigation carried certain risks beyond that also. Breaking into the police station meant they had crossed the lines of legality now too.

"I'm sorry," Felicity whispered.

"What? No! That's not what I meant!"

"I know; I'm in your head, remember? But I still am sorry."

Adam's hold on her tightened. It felt good being this close to him again.

Memories of their first kiss flooded her mind again. Imagery of their lovemaking followed immediately after.

ALPHA SQUAD: FRIENDS AND FOES

She turned slightly to face him again. They were in perfect sync; there he was already, looking at her. Waiting. His lips were slightly parted, as were hers.

She wanted him again. To feel the ultimate bond.

They were so close. Each breath of his caressed her lips.

Felicity closed her eyes and waited.

But the kiss never happened.

Instead, a loud bang on the door ruined the mood. Followed by the very last phrase either one of them wanted to hear right now.

"Open up! Police!"

Shit. Adam's thoughts started to race. *I'm pretty sure nobody saw me; why the hell are they here now?*

It's that horrible detective, I recognize his voice, Felicity thought.

Adam got up to answer the door, but Felicity grabbed his arm at the very last moment.

No, this is my house. I should do it.

It would be too easy to freak out now. To assume that their fact-finding mission into the police station had been discovered somehow. But what if it was just a coincidence? They had to play it cool until they knew what this was really about.

"Just a second, please!" Felicity called out.

Felicity piled all the files they'd stolen into Adam's arms and herded him toward the back of the house. *Stay out of view. I'll handle it. We don't need him finding us here together.*

Adam hesitated for a moment, but then he did as told.

Only then did Felicity open the front door.

It was Detective Nye sporting one of his sinister grins.

"Felicity Weir, I have a warrant for your arrest."

Felicity took a step back in shock. They were here just for *her*? Perhaps it wasn't related to the break-in at all, then.

"What on earth for?" she stammered.

Please! Stay out of sight or they'll get you too! she thought.

I'll get you out. I promise, Adam responded.

Detective Nye held up a sheet of paper.

"Four counts of animal cruelty, tampering with evidence, obstruction, and… murder!"

Felicity had no words.

So they were going to pin all of this on her. After Adam and she had tried so hard and come so close to discovering the truth. Unbelievable.

"You're not serious! Next you'll tell me I set the fire at the shifter camp also."

"We can't prove that," Nye countered. "Yet."

"That doesn't even make any sense."

"I'm sure you'll explain how it all fits together back at the station during your interrogation."

"I don't believe it," Felicity mumbled, as Detective Nye grabbed her by the wrists and secured her in cuffs. Then he patted her down, taking his own sweet time. As if she needed any weapon if she really wanted to hurt the man. It would take just one focused shift on her part and her instincts would do the rest.

If he hurts you, I'll kill him! Adam's thoughts entered her mind from across the house. Their connection was intensifying; earlier, she wouldn't have been able to hear him from more than a couple of feet away.

Please, Adam. Stay back! Felicity thought. If he saw this guy with his hands all over her, who knew what might happen. He'd get arrested too, and for good reason. At least one of them should be out to continue the investigation to clear her name. The Sevenoaks police department couldn't be trusted with the task, clearly.

They couldn't even look beyond their own prejudices, it seemed.

Who the hell had signed off on her arrest anyway? Based on what evidence? Adam had gathered all he could from the station and at first glance, nothing seemed to point at her. It didn't make any sense.

She could do nothing but shake her head as the detective pushed her through her front door and down to the pavement, where a police car waited, flashing lights and all.

"Mind your head," Detective Nye spoke in a low growl, as he shoved her into the backseat.

It was surreal, being driven through the town where she had lived all her life in the back of a police car. In cuffs, no less. If her parents could see her now, they'd die of embarrassment. She'd get through this, with Adam's help. She hadn't even *done* anything, well, except driving the getaway car after the police station break-in.

Sooner or later, the police had to see that too. Unless…

No, that was too devious. She stared at the two men in the front cab of the car. One in uniform; she had never seen him before. And the other was Detective Nye…

Surely the cops in this town weren't so crooked that they'd pin this on her with false evidence?

Felicity took a deep breath. She'd get to the station and demand legal representation. And then, this whole mess would have to work itself out somehow. Plus, there was always Adam, who wouldn't rest until she was in the clear. She wasn't on her own anymore. Everything would be okay…

Right?

CHAPTER TWELVE

Adam had come out of hiding the moment the door to Felicity's house had clicked shut. What followed was a painful hour or so of pacing back and forth as he tried to wrap his mind around what had just happened.

They had arrested her for the murders. Based on what evidence?

It was so surreal, he couldn't even begin to understand it.

Just being separated from her under such terrible circumstances was driving him insane. It was an epic battle of mind over heart, as he tried his very best to rationalize what had happened and how to fix it, versus his animal side that just wanted to break free and go on a rampage.

If the detective came back here now, he would only leave in an ambulance; that much was certain.

But this wasn't about *him*. It wasn't about the detective or Adam's ego.

This was about Felicity.

Although Adam was the one who had taken the risks, and actually broken the law, for some reason, she was their prime target. What had she done to the police to make them so suspicious, even hostile? Detective Nye's notes identified her as a person of interest, but his reasoning wasn't nailed down in the notes. He had found out about her true nature, of course. But then again, he knew that Adam was a bear shifter too. As were half the residents of the refugee camp. So that alone could not have been his sole reason for zeroing in on Felicity.

Academics weren't Adam's strong suit, but he did his best to work his way through all the material he had copied at the station.

Every last report, every bit of evidence the cops had catalogued. He looked through it all and studied it harder than he had ever studied anything his whole life.

And it was all infuriatingly vague and inconclusive. How on earth had they found a judge to sign off on an arrest warrant based on this non-evidence?

There was something fishy going on here, and it was up to him to find out exactly what.

Adam slammed the file shut and got up. He'd promised he'd get Felicity out of this, and that was exactly what he was going to do. But first of all, he had to make sure she was okay. Who knew what they were doing to her back at the station.

So Adam packed up all the files and did the only thing he could think of. He borrowed Felicity's car and headed to the inn, where the squad would have called it a night hours ago.

Eric would be disappointed in him if he told him the truth, but he was still his brother. There had to be some loyalty there, surely.

As he navigated his way through the dark, empty

corridors of the inn, looking for Eric, Adam wasn't surprised that his nose led him straight to the major's room. Of course he was in there.

"Psst, Eric," Adam whispered.

He could just knock on the door, but then he'd tip off the major to his presence here, and that wasn't his intention. No, he kept his volume low enough that only a shifter's super-sensitive hearing would pick up on it.

"Eric, I need to talk to you," he said.

Sure enough, there was a rustling noise inside the room, followed by the click of the lock.

"What the hell?" Eric complained under his breath. "This is hardly appropriate, you coming here!"

"Look, I don't care what the two of you get up to. I'm not one to judge. But shit has hit the fan and I need your help."

Eric turned to glance back at the dark room. Deep, regular breaths signaled that the major was oblivious to Adam's visit.

"I'm not sure how I can help. You've made your choice; you're off the team."

Adam nodded. "Yeah, whatever. But you're not. And I have some stuff here that you might want to see."

Eric stepped out and carefully shut the door behind him. "Okay, but you'd better not be messing with me."

"Where can we talk freely?" Adam asked.

Eric led the way to his own room, just down the

hallway.

Once inside, he gestured at Adam to sit on the bed. "Go on. Tell me what's going on now?"

Adam handed Eric the file. "This is all the evidence the cops have."

Eric frowned. "Do I even want to know how you got this?"

Adam shook his head. "The point is, this is everything, including stuff they never shared with us." He retrieved the plastic bag with the metal shard Felicity had found during her initial visit to the third murder scene. "And this was left behind at the scene of the third murder."

"And what exactly do you want from me now?" Eric asked, while holding up the bag against the light to inspect it more closely.

"They've arrested Felicity," Adam said.

Eric inhaled sharply. "What are the charges?"

"Animal cruelty, tampering with evidence, murder."

"Shit."

"Yeah."

"Okay, thanks for this. I'll mobilize the team and get to work. And I'll have someone check in to the station to make sure Felicity is okay." Eric's outrage sounded genuine.

They had always had their issues, but now that push came to shove, Adam was relieved to find that he could count on his brother.

"Thanks, bro."

ALPHA SQUAD: FRIENDS AND FOES

With that, Adam got up and left. Alpha Squad would work the official investigation, but there was still no room for him here. And his nature didn't allow him to sit around and wait. He would continue to gather evidence in parallel himself. The more heads working on this case simultaneously, the better their chances of getting Felicity out.

---·---

The interrogation had gone on for many hours; Felicity wasn't sure how long exactly. Mostly it was Detective Nye in the room on his own, but occasionally his mostly silent partner had sat in as well. Other than that, the police station was quiet; she couldn't detect any other human presence in the building no matter how hard she listened for it. That made sense, of course, considering just hours earlier Adam had gotten into the building completely unseen. At that time, not even the detectives had been here.

She wondered what had mobilized them at such an ungodly hour.

The more the questions continued, the more Felicity felt her patience wear down. At least they seemed oblivious to the break-in, for now. That was one positive Felicity tried to focus on. But there was little else to feed her optimism. In truth, she was exhausted.

The same questions, over and over.

Why had she killed those three people? Who were her associates? Nye seemed convinced that shifter or not, she would not have been capable of doing so much damage all on her own. *If only he knew exactly what an angry shifter was capable of, he might sing a different tune.* How was the shifter camp involved?

Felicity's throat was getting sore answering identically every time. She hadn't done it. She didn't know. She was innocent and to the best of her knowledge, so were the refugees.

Finally, it seemed like the detective was getting tired himself. He left without a word, and she was alone.

Where was her solicitor, anyway? She'd asked for one multiple times already, but nobody had come. And the interrogation had continued regardless.

After what felt like an age, the door to the little room she was in opened, and she braced herself for another round of bullshit questions.

It wasn't Detective Nye this time, though. It was the other guy.

"I thought you could use a cup of tea," he said, placing a plastic cup down in front of her.

She eyed the pale milky liquid suspiciously, then looked up at him.

"What are you then, the good cop?"

The man pressed his lips together. Again, there was something about him that she couldn't quite identify. A look in his eyes. Remorse? Guilt? He walked across the room and reached for the camera mounted in the corner that was pointing right at Felicity. He pressed a button and the red light next to the lens switched off.

"I suppose you could say that."

"Well, I'm not interested in you buttering me up. I'm not going to confess. I have nothing to confess to," Felicity said, and folded her arms.

She stared at the man to make her point. Hopefully, she looked a lot more confident than she felt. Truthfully, she was close to the edge. She could cry. But that would just make Detective Nasty happy.

"You know, I never wanted this," Detective McMillan said.

"Well that makes two of us. You people just keep pointing fingers at me and my community. But you know what you don't have? Proof."

"Actually…"

Felicity felt her eyes widen, even though she tried her best to keep her expression neutral. So they did have something on her? How was that even possible?"

"I shouldn't be telling you this, but I feel like we've gotten to know each other a little bit these last few weeks."

What the hell?

"I'm not sure I understand. We've hardly spoken a word until now."

"That's not *entirely* accurate." The detective glanced over his shoulder, even though there was obviously nobody else in the room with them.

"Oh?" Felicity frowned.

"Those phone calls…"

Finally, something clicked into place. The way he spoke, combined with him making every possible effort not to interact with her in person… he was her anonymous tipster!

"*You've* been calling me? Holy sh—" Felicity tried to catch her breath. "I mean, why? Why feed me information? Have you been trying to set me up all this time?"

The man shook his head. "No, I've been trying to help you. Because it was quite obvious from the start that nobody here was going to look deeply enough at these attacks to find out the truth. They just wanted to believe the explanation they found the most appealing, you know? They never looked beyond the camp and whoever works there."

Wow. She wanted to believe it. To see this as a ray of hope in what had to be one of her darkest days ever. But how did she know he was even telling the truth? How could she be sure he wasn't just tricking her now, after running some kind of trace on her phone and finding out about the calls that way?

"I don't believe you," Felicity said, all of a sudden painfully aware of how much her eyes stung. *Stop it,* anything not to cry right now in front of this cop!

"I can prove it, but you'll have to watch me very

closely," the man said.

"Look, Detective McMillan, was it? I don't know what your game is, but I'm not about to be tricked into stuff by you pretending to be my friend. And what about the legal representation I asked for hours ago?"

"Call me Sean," he said.

Then something very odd happened.

A human might not have been able to detect the change in him, but Felicity did. It was uncanny. A flutter came over the detective's skin. And for a split second, it seemed like he was sprouting fur. But how could that be? His scent was unmistakably human, and yet here he was, very nearly allowing himself to transform in front of her.

"You're… I don't believe it. How is that even possible?" Felicity mumbled.

"I know. I appear totally human."

"So how come you're not?"

"My mother was a bear shifter. My father was human."

Felicity took a moment to let this new information sink in. She'd heard of mixed couples in the area, very few of them. Toward the end of her stint with the Alliance, just before shifters had *come out*, the higher-ups had ordered Felicity and her team to make a list of any mixed couples they could find, as so-called impure unions had been outlawed. The new rules did not gel with her own code of ethics, so Felicity had fudged her data. But even then, she had never once heard of a mixed couple with offspring.

"You're a hybrid," she concluded.

Sean McMillan nodded. "Don't tell anyone. Especially not my partner. I never planned for this to come out, but under the current circumstances… I thought you should know."

Felicity's heart was beating so hard now, she had to wonder if he could hear it. She had so many questions, it was difficult to pick the one that was going to be her first.

"I won't, but—"

Unfortunately, before she had the chance to ask him anything at all, the door swung open, revealing Detective Nye with a predatory scowl on his face.

He was back. But even though today had been tough, this new knowledge had given Felicity the boost she so desperately needed. She now knew she wouldn't break.

Not now, not ever.

"Oh, you're already here, Sean. Good. Let's try this again. Ms. Weir, why don't you tell us about how you brutally murdered three people?"

"I'm not saying a word until my lawyer gets here." Felicity folded her arms and stared straight ahead. Armed with the knowledge that she had at least one person on her side inside the police station, she was ready to fight even harder.

Detective Nye sighed deeply and folded his hands. "Sean, why don't you go see if the public defender has arrived yet?"

ALPHA SQUAD: FRIENDS AND FOES

Sean McMillan shot a final sympathetic look in her direction before leaving the room again.

CHAPTER THIRTEEN

———•———

As hard as Adam had tried to stay focused, he couldn't stay away from the police station. So that was where he waited now, uncertain about what was next.

Dawn had come and gone, and the town was starting to wake up from its early morning slumber.

But Adam had no interest in the passersby, or the shops that were starting to open their shutters. His eyes were fixed on the station.

Felicity was in there, and she was counting on him to free her.

That he had handed the files of the murder investigation over to Eric was only a small consolation. Actually, he felt like he had just passed the buck and wasn't pulling his weight anymore, which totally hadn't been his intention.

But no matter how he felt, he knew it didn't matter. Nothing did, except Felicity's wellbeing and freedom. That was why he was here; staking out the police station in a last ditch attempt to be useful in getting her out.

He didn't even know what he was waiting for exactly. Was he planning on sneaking in and trying to see her? That would be stupid and reckless and possibly get both of them into even more trouble. No, he was just… waiting.

A familiar figure appeared at the main door of the

ALPHA SQUAD: FRIENDS AND FOES

station. The horrible detective. He rummaged around in his pocket and retrieved a packet of cigarettes, lighting one and taking a deep drag.

Adam's eyes narrowed. It would be too easy to overpower the man and fight his way inside to rescue Felicity. How many cops would even be here at this hour?

But Adam resisted and instead continued to observe the detective as he smoked. When his cigarette was almost finished, he twitched subtly, as though something had startled him. Had he noticed Adam staring at him from across the road?

The man threw his cigarette down and put it out with the heel of his shoe, then he reached for something else in his pocket: a phone.

It was already ringing; the sound of it echoed against the surrounding buildings now as it grew louder and louder.

Adam held his breath and listened carefully.

"Yeah, this is Nye. No problem. I can be there in ten minutes."

The detective hung up and checked the street as though he was conscious of being watched. When he had seemingly satisfied himself that he was on his own, he started to walk resolutely toward the small parking lot located next to the police station, and got into one of the cars.

Adam was certain that this phone call and the meeting

discussed within were significant somehow. If it was all just routine, surely the detective wouldn't acted so suspiciously on the way to his vehicle.

So now it was just a matter of continuing to follow him without being seen… Adam swiftly moved across the street and got into Felicity's car, waiting patiently until the detective had pulled out of the parking and progressed some distance up the road, before turning on the engine himself and joining the traffic.

There were few cars on the road, although the traffic did get busier as they passed through the main market area of Sevenoaks.

Adam took care not to attract attention to himself, and even allowed multiple vehicles to join ahead of him to give some distance between his car and the detective's. So far, all seemed normal. The detective was driving along calmly, as though he was unaware of Adam's presence.

Once they got to the outskirts of town, things became more difficult. The traffic thinned out, forcing Adam to fall back further. Unfortunately, that meant he was unable to react quickly to any change in direction. A couple of turns through twisty narrow country roads, and the detective's car was nowhere to be seen.

Adam pulled over and punched the steering in frustration. This had been his chance, and he'd blown it by letting the detective get away.

He took a deep breath and forced his anger back down. This wasn't the time to lose control. He still had work to do.

Just as he turned on his indicator, preparing to head back into town, a pair of large black SUVs passed him by. He only saw inside for a split second, but immediately recognized one of the occupants who was looking out the rear window.

Victor Domnall. Leader of the militant anti-shifter organization the Sons of Domnall, which was responsible for numerous shifter deaths and disappearances for multiple decades, even before mainstream society had found out about their kind.

What was the arch nemesis of all shifterkind himself doing here, driving along an empty country road only moments after Detective Nye had passed by in the same direction?

Adam wasn't sure what this meant, only that it couldn't be a coincidence.

He acted quickly and gave chase. No way would he let these people get away as well.

He followed the two-car procession through the twisty section of road up ahead, until they pulled into an overgrown path off to the left. Adam continued on straight and pulled up on the soft berm next to the road just out of view, beyond the next turn. He'd have to go the rest of the way on foot.

Adam did his best not to make too much noise as he cut through the overgrown field that separated him from the property where Victor Domnall's vehicle had turned off. A shifter would have heard him coming, but a bunch of humans? Not a chance.

Finally, he reached a chain link fence. On the other side, he could see the two black SUVs, as well as Detective Nye's car.

The men stood in a cluster in the center between the three vehicles. Adam listened as best he could, but they were just a bit too far away, and the rustle of the leaves overhead covered a lot of their conversation.

Still, this was significant. Adam found his phone in his pocket and took numerous pictures of the gathering in front of him, zooming in to the men's faces as best he could and finally taking a video of it as well.

Who knew, this could be important evidence. He would hand it over to Eric as soon as they got out of here.

One of the men who had accompanied Victor Domnall stepped away and reached for something in the backseat of one of the SUVs. Adam held his breath. Was the meeting going bad?

But it wasn't a weapon which the man had retrieved, it was a medium sized brown envelope.

Adam kept the phone as steady as possible while continuing to videotape the exchange.

What was it? A pay off? And what exactly had the detective done to earn it?

The detective and Victor Domnall shook hands, then each returned to their respective vehicles. Adam put the phone away and darted back across the field to where he had parked Felicity's car.

This wasn't over yet. He had to figure out what was in the brown packet Domnall had given to the detective. Whatever it was, perhaps it would blow this case wide open and set Felicity free.

Adam pulled out onto the road, stopping just short of a turn that would shield him from view, and rolled down his window. He waited there just for a moment until he heard the other vehicles drive away. He crept up around the turn and could just about make out the rear of Detective Nye's car. Now or never.

The drive back into town was easier; at least Adam had a fairly good idea of the direction they were headed in, so he didn't have to follow too closely.

Right until the detective took an unexpected right turn.

Adam gripped the steering wheel tighter and waited feverishly for an opening in the traffic.

Where the hell was he going? This wasn't the way to the police station!

Finally, Adam could make the turn as well. It led into a residential area which looked kind of familiar.

Detective Nye's car was nowhere to be seen.

Adam kept going until he hit a T-junction. No sign of his prey to the left or the right.

Someone pulled up behind him and honked their horn, forcing him to move quickly, so he randomly decided to turn left.

As he continued through the narrow road, lined with apartment buildings on one side and family homes on the other, it dawned on Adam where they were.

Felicity lived just around the corner.

Could it be?

Adam pulled into the nearest parking spot and got out of the car, cutting through a children's playground and a small park on the way to Felicity's house.

Detective Nye was already there.

Adam positioned himself behind some shrubbery across the street and watched as the detective fumbled with the lock of the front door.

Adam pulled out his phone again and recorded the man's every move. It didn't take Nye long to pick the lock and break in.

Detective Nye checked over his shoulder once before entering Felicity's home, the suspicious brown packet he'd received from Victor Domnall in hand.

Adam got out of hiding and sprinted across the road and checked the windows facing the pavement. The kitchenette window allowed for the best possible view inside; luckily, the curtains weren't drawn.

From here, Adam could see Detective Nye pull something out of the envelope; unfortunately, the latter had his back turned so the exact item was out of view.

He then rummaged around in a chest of drawers in the living room and stuffed the envelope's contents deep inside.

That was Adam's cue to move yet again. He ran around the side of the apartment block and concealed himself in a stairwell until he heard the detective shut the door of Felicity's flat behind him and start his car. Adam breathed a sigh of relief when he was on his own again. At least he thought he was.

Upon turning around, he found a pair of light blue eyes looking up at him in awe.

"Well hello there, little man," Adam stammered. Usually, he was much better with kids, but not now, when he was so clearly caught in the act of spying on someone.

The boy, who didn't look older than five or six, blinked a few times and continued to hold on tightly to the football in his little hands.

"I'm not allowed to talk to strangers," he said.

"That's good. You shouldn't." Adam attempted to smile.

"My mommy says they took Felicity away. The police did. She says Felicity has done a very bad thing," the boy said.

"You know Felicity?" Adam asked.

He nodded. "She's nice. I hope they let her go."

Adam nodded. "Yeah. Me too. Well, she's asked me to pick up something from her flat. So I'd better not make her wait."

The boy nodded gravely. "My mommy hates it when I

make her wait."

"You be good now, okay?" Adam said.

"Tell Felicity I don't believe she did anything bad," the boy called after him.

Well, at least they had someone else on their side, even if it was just a little boy from her neighborhood. Adam approached Felicity's place and was about to check that nobody was watching when he remembered the keys in his pocket. He'd picked them up on the way out after she was taken. To hell with everyone; he wasn't breaking in! He was here with her permission.

It didn't take Adam long to find the mysterious items the detective had stashed in Felicity's living room. But what he found was so damning, it very nearly took his breath away.

He took a few pictures of the entire drawer, and close-ups of the evidence itself. Then he made a phone call.

"Eric, I have evidence of Detective Nye framing Felicity for the murders. I'm going to send you the address. Hurry. Bring the team." Adam didn't wait for any acknowledgment, just cut the call.

From a straight up surveillance mission, this had escalated into something much bigger. By sheer luck, Adam had achieved a breakthrough in the case.

The worst was almost over.

CHAPTER FOURTEEN

———◆———

Felicity had spent hours by herself in one of the holding cells of the station ever since the interrogation had ended. Or had been paused, whatever it was. She still had no idea what time it was or long she had been in custody.

All she could do was lie down on the cot in the corner and stare at the ceiling, counting the cracks in the plaster.

Since her short chat with Sean McMillan, her unexpected ally, she had been able to survive the rest of the questioning with her head held high. And it seemed that Detective Nye's patience had worn thin instead; she hadn't seen him ever since he left the interrogation ages ago.

Perhaps he had given up?

Another person she hadn't seen was her lawyer, whoever that was meant to be. Clearly the police weren't too concerned about her civil rights. Whether that was because they were generally incompetent or because being a shifter made her a second-rate citizen, she couldn't be sure.

Either way, this could only last for so long, until someone had to intervene. If not Adam, then surely whoever was in charge of this sad excuse for a police force. And when that happened, she would have her revenge, ensuring that the horrible detective got into trouble for everything he'd done to her.

Felicity had run out of ceiling to inspect, so she turned onto her side and stared at the wall instead. Her mind wandered; no point dwelling on the injustice that was happening to her in here. She thought about her relationship with Adam instead. What a whirlwind it had been.

She'd dated before, obviously, but nothing could compare. Not every shifter found their true mate, but when they did, the connection was undeniable. It was a force of nature that could not be negotiated or argued with.

Although she was in here, she knew he was out there doing his best to fix things. And deep inside her heart, she knew that he would be successful.

Funnily, even though they had consummated their relationship already, she didn't know all that much about him. She'd tried to get more of an insight into who he was the other night, but their conversation had been cut short by the arrival of Detective Nye with her arrest warrant.

But at the same time, that didn't really matter. Felicity knew that he only wanted what was best for her. She could trust him with her life.

Similarly, had the tables been turned, she would have done anything for him.

This knowledge was a huge comfort to her.

That was when it hit her. This feeling of reassurance, that everything was going to be okay—it had gradually grown stronger just during the last few minutes. She wasn't alone anymore; Adam had arrived. He was in the building somewhere.

She sat upright with her feet up on the edge of the bed and wrapped her arms around her legs. If he was inside, that could only mean one thing; he had discovered something that would help, and she would soon get out of here.

Felicity closed her eyes and focused on his presence. Yes, he was definitely getting closer.

She thought she could hear voices elsewhere in the building, but it wasn't clear enough to understand what they were saying.

Where are you? Are you okay? Adam's thoughts infiltrated her own.

She swallowed the lump in her throat. *Yes, I'm fine. I'm so glad you made it.*

The longer she waited, the harder her heart hammered away in her chest. She was getting giddy and impatient. This cell seemed so small and oppressive all of a sudden.

Relax, Adam will be here soon.

Sure enough, she could hear a heavy door being unlocked some distance away, followed by multiple pairs of footsteps.

Adam came into view, along with Detective McMillan.

Felicity jumped up and approached the door of her cell. *Finally!*

"Ms. Weir, in light of some brand new evidence, I'm releasing you effective immediately. You are free to go." Detective McMillan smiled at her.

"Thank you, Sean," Felicity said.

Adam raised an eyebrow. *You're on a first name basis with this guy?*

Felicity suppressed a smile. *It's a long story. What did you find out?*

She followed Adam out of the holding area and into the main part of the police station, near the interrogation rooms where she'd been held earlier. All the while, he telepathically explained exactly what had happened. From watching Detective Nye make the phone call outside the station early in the morning, to following him across town, right until he uncovered the evidence that he had concealed in Felicity's flat.

What was it? Felicity asked.

Adam, who had been eager to explain everything so far, now hesitated.

You'd rather not know; trust me.

Actually, I do want to know. Especially if it was in my living room!

"Why don't the both of you wait here, while I get the paperwork for your release ready? I won't be long," Sean said.

Felicity nodded, then turned to face Adam again. *Are you going to tell me what you found or not?*

Fine!

ALPHA SQUAD: FRIENDS AND FOES

Rather than explain it, Adam opened his mind to her so that she could see exactly what he had seen at her house that morning. It was like a movie; first images of the detective going through her things, then a close up of the cabinet in her living room. Far toward the back of the top drawer, Felicity could see a small collection of see-through plastic baggies, like the kind you see drug dealers use on TV. Inside each of them, a blood-stained lock of hair.

It was like a little collection of trophies belonging to a serial killer.

Felicity shuddered at the thought. This was how Victor Domnall tried to present shifters to the world? Like scary killers, who keep track of their body count with a catalog of hair clippings? How outrageous.

Felicity wanted to believe that nobody would take that seriously, but after everything that had happened, especially the arson attack on the shifter camp, she wasn't so sure anymore. People seemed eager to accept any story as long as it fit into their preconceived notions.

About that fire, Adam's thoughts entered hers again.

Yeah?

It turns out the same people were behind it. Domnall's guys. One of them was proudly bragging about it when Eric arrested them.

She sat back, stunned, and let the information sink in for a bit. *Domnall's men did everything? Save for Detective Nasty, nobody in town had anything to do with it?*

It looks like that.

That should have been a relief, only Felicity couldn't quite believe it yet. The whole situation seemed utterly surreal; like she was about to wake up and find herself back in that stupid holding cell again.

Trust me, this is really over. Adam put his arm around her.

She tried to focus on breathing deeply and calmly. Her entire body was still tense, and her mind was still racing as she tried to put the last pieces of the puzzle together. She wanted to believe Adam, of course, but she was too frazzled. Sleep deprivation was taking its toll.

"Are we going to be done here soon?" Adam called out.

A split second later, Sean McMillan stuck his head around one of the open doorways within view. "Almost done, I do apologize for the delay!"

Just as McMillan vanished again, the main entrance door burst open, revealing a grumpy looking Detective Nye with Adam's brother, Eric, right behind him.

Felicity kept her eyes locked on the detective, who glared at her as Eric proceeded to shove him straight past her position. *Serves him right.*

"Don't think you people have won, just because you arrested me!" Detective Nye said. "This isn't over! It will never be over! The Sons will not rest until your kind is eradicated!"

Felicity held her breath, but didn't respond. After her first one-to-one talk with the man, it was obvious that his prejudices against shifters ran deep. It wasn't a huge

ALPHA SQUAD: FRIENDS AND FOES

surprise to discover now that his loyalties lay firmly with Victor Domnall and his hateful organization.

The only unusual thing about this was his apparent willingness to admit to it. Most Sons of Domnall members Felicity had heard of being captured during her old days at the Alliance never confessed to anything.

She shrugged.

It didn't matter. If he wanted to go down screaming, that was his right.

Just as Adam's brother and Detective Nasty disappeared through one of the doors leading to the holding cells, the rest of Alpha Squad arrived.

The mood in the station shifted instantly; policemen that had been focused deeply on their work just a second earlier completely stopped whatever they were doing. Conversations were interrupted, phone calls went unanswered.

"Major Williams." A portly man with gray hair approached and shook her hand. "I apologize deeply for what has happened here. We had no idea of Detective Nye's involvement, or we wouldn't have allowed for things to escalate as they have."

The major did not answer immediately; instead, she approached Felicity and Adam.

"Chief Inspector Huddersfield," she said, raising her voice. "It is not me you ought to apologize to!"

She nodded first at Felicity, then at Adam.

"Good work, soldier."

"Thank you, Ma'am," Adam responded.

"Felicity Weir, it's a pleasure to finally meet you," Major Williams said as she shook her hand.

Felicity nodded. She had been suspicious about Alpha Squad's purpose in town from the moment they'd arrived, but perhaps they weren't so bad after all. Shame they kicked Adam out because of her…

"If you don't mind, I have some questions I'd like to ask you," the major said.

Adam straightened himself and was about to protest, when Major Williams raised her hand to calm him down. "Don't worry, not right now. You've been through a lot. I would love the chance to clear up a few things with you, though. Whenever it's convenient."

Felicity nodded. That was fair enough.

You don't have to if you don't want to, Adam thought.

It's fine. Perhaps I'll ask her a few things as well.

Major Williams nodded at the two of them and marched straight into what appeared to be the chief inspector's office. The lecture that followed was loud enough that even the humans in the room could clearly hear it.

Meanwhile, McMillan returned, holding a stack of papers.

"All done. You are free to go, Felicity Weir."

She smiled at him gratefully and tugged at Adam's arm. "Let's go then," she said.

ALPHA SQUAD: FRIENDS AND FOES

They were almost all the way out of the station when she stopped in her tracks. "The refugees! Has anyone checked into the refugees while I was in here?"

Adam pulled her close to him. "Don't worry, Blackwood has been spending some time there since the fire, just helping out with the rebuild. And anyway, it's only been a day and a half. I'm sure they've been fine."

Felicity breathed a sigh of relief.

Adam led the way out, pushing the main doors of the police station open. The square outside was abuzz with activity. But they weren't just protesters that waited in front of the station; there were camera crews and reporters, all rushing up to Felicity and Adam, unleashing a barrage of questions their way.

"No comment! We have nothing to say!" Adam declared, as he guided Felicity through the frenzy.

Just great. This is the last thing I needed right now, Felicity thought.

Don't worry. The major will hold a press conference tomorrow, and everything will be sorted, Adam tried to reassure her.

I hope so.

CHAPTER FIFTEEN

---◆---

It had taken longer than he would have wanted, but finally, Felicity was free. After a quiet night in reflecting on everything and sharing their respective sides of the story, Adam and Felicity were back at the police station. Not as persons of interest or even suspects, but as witnesses to the press conference the major had promised the journalists.

Adam glanced over at Felicity as she stood by his side just a few paces away from the podium; her brown hair glistened in the midday sun. How beautiful she was. How radiant, despite everything she had been through.

He also exchanged a look and a nod of understanding with Eric, who stood directly in front of the crowd. He, as well as the rest of Alpha Squad, had been instrumental in getting Felicity released based on the evidence Adam had seen Detective Nye plant at her house.

The entire scene, the team preparing for its first press conference in front of a crowd of people outside the police station, reminded Adam a lot of the brief ceremony that had marked the end of Alpha Squad's boot camp training. Only this time, their audience didn't consist of army and government officials, only reporters and ordinary citizens who had come to find out exactly what was happening in their little town.

ALPHA SQUAD: FRIENDS AND FOES

The microphone emitted a horrible screeching noise as Chief Inspector Huddersfield pointed it up closer to his mouth.

"I am pleased to announce that we have a number of suspects in custody, who are have already confessed to their role in the recent murders that have shocked our town." He glanced over at Major Williams and hesitated.

"We started the investigation expecting to find only one or at most a few culprits acting on their own. What we found was a much wider conspiracy, involving members of my own department."

A whisper passed through the crowd.

Although Huddersfield had named no names, everyone knew he was talking about Detective Nye. As soon as Alpha Squad had moved in and arrested the man at his home, the story had spread through the town like wildfire. The journalists would have found many willing to talk and give their side of the story; everyone had been very quick to cut all ties, actual as well as perceived, to Nye and the two Sons of Domnall members he had identified as being behind the murders.

"Although the worst is now over, we must not make light of what this investigation has uncovered. My very own department, embroiled in a scandal of corruption, which led to the unlawful detention of a citizen and loyal servant of Sevenoaks, Felicity Weir. I hereby wish to take full responsibility and apologize on behalf of Kent Police.

Your rights were violated on my watch, and I know my words can hardly begin to make up for all you went through."

Take responsibility, huh? It's all just talk. If he truly felt responsible, he ought to resign, Adam thought.

Felicity squeezed his hand. *Let it be. It's over.*

"I also want to take this opportunity to thank the fine men and women of Alpha Squad, who were instrumental in unraveling this case," Huddersfield continued. "It was through your hard work and cooperation with my department that the truth could finally be uncovered and the culprits brought to justice. I salute you."

Chief Inspector Huddersfield stepped back, allowing Major Williams to approach the podium.

"Thank you, Chief Inspector, we appreciate your kind words. I also want to take this opportunity to highlight that Alpha Squad would have been unable to solve the case without the dedication and hard work of the local police. Sure, Alpha Squad has been conceived as a special government task force to handle shifter related incidents nationwide, but we cannot work in a vacuum, neither do we wish to replace local law enforcement. Our role is purely supportive, to share our special training and shifter related knowledge with local authorities in resolving crimes relating to or affecting the shifter community. On that note, I wish to highlight that with the help of local Detective McMillan, we have managed to resolve the case of the horrible attack on the shifter camp a few days ago.

ALPHA SQUAD: FRIENDS AND FOES

Once again, suspects are in custody, and they're ready to talk."

The major as well as the chief inspector had been vague on purpose while announcing the arrests of everyone involved in the attacks on both the human and shifter population of Sevenoaks. They could not share too much information about an ongoing investigation for fear of jeopardizing it, but at least Adam and the rest of the team knew the truth.

Victor Domnall had been behind it all. His presence in town had indeed not been a coincidence; after sending in some of his henchmen to start a terror campaign on the human citizens of the town, he had come in to reap the benefits by making speeches and stirring up hatred against the shifters. But save for handing the evidence that was meant to convict Felicity to the crooked detective, he had not gotten his own hands dirty. And even the pictures showing the exchange were not sufficient to hold up in court; all you could see was a sealed envelope, and the actual evidence was not within view.

The leader of the Sons of Domnall was a slippery fellow indeed. Apparently, he had already left town in a hurry as soon as the arrests had taken place.

But Alpha Squad would not give up so easily. It did not matter to them where Victor Domnall was; they would return to base and continue to investigate behind the scenes, waiting for the illustrious man to make his next move.

It wasn't ideal, but it was all they could do. Sooner or later, he would make a mistake. It would only be a matter of time before Alpha Squad would find something that proved his direct involvement in an anti-shifter crime and put the man away once and for all.

"What about reports that the victims were mauled by a large animal, say, a bear?" one of the journalists called out.

Major Williams shook her head. "Rumors, I'm afraid. The victims were stabbed. In fact, I have the murder weapon right here."

She leaned down and picked up a strange looking metal contraption off the ground behind the podium and held it up for everyone to see.

Journalists and civilians alike gasped in shock. It was a scary looking thing, an intricate set of blades and pulleys that could be operated by hand to simulate either a set of claws or a jaw full of sharp teeth. It was easy to imagine just how much damage this thing would do to a human body.

"I trust this answers any remaining concerns. If there are no more questions, my team and I would like to get back to work," Major Williams ended the press conference.

The journalists started to disperse; no doubt they were all eager to report on the announcements made in the conference. Meanwhile, Alpha Squad, along with Felicity and the local police, headed back into the station.

Once inside and shielded from any remaining prying

eyes, Felicity took Major Williams aside. "I wanted to apologize too."

The major turned around, her eyebrows raised in surprise. "What for?"

"I jumped to conclusions about the squad and felt compelled to continue investigating things myself. I should have trusted that your team would look at the case objectively and draw the right conclusions."

The Major stared at Adam for a moment, then looked at Felicity again and shook her hand. "Well, perhaps we should have done a better job in the first place. It took us a while to follow the right lead, but at least we got there in the end. Together."

Adam nodded, and rested his hand on Felicity's shoulder.

"Mr. King, I very much hope that this experience here has not permanently impacted your involvement with the team?"

Adam raised an eyebrow. "Not at all. Does this mean I'm back in?"

"I understand that what happened here was a one-off that could be blamed on extenuating circumstances…" Major Williams's voice trailed off.

A one-off indeed. It wasn't every day that you stumbled across your one true mate while in the midst of a murder investigation.

"It certainly won't happen again," Adam said.

The major glanced across at Eric, who had been observing their exchange from across the buzzing police station, and smiled subtly.

"Very well then. Welcome back to the team."

Major Williams shook his hand to seal the deal.

Adam felt Felicity's heart rate surge in excitement. *Congratulations! I was worried I'd cost you your position on the team.*

Even if, it's only a job, Adam thought. That wasn't totally true, though. This job, unlike any other he'd ever had, actually meant something. It was meaningful, and it had the potential of being satisfying as well. That didn't make it more important than Felicity, but still. It was a relief that in the end, he didn't have to choose after all.

"We leave in the morning, back to base," Major Williams said, then observed the happy couple for a moment. "I suppose you'll want some time off?" she asked Adam.

Adam nodded. "Just a day or so, to sort things out here."

Adam and Felicity exchanged a smile. It had been a tumultuous few days; it would be such a relief to get away from everything and everyone for a little while. After that, they'd sort out exactly how their future together would look.

They were about to leave together, when the major cleared her throat.

"Actually, Ms. Weir, there's something I've been

thinking about which you might be able to help me with."

"Oh?" Felicity asked. "What's that?"

"The refugee camp. You know those families like nobody else. The way everybody spoke about you, you seemed to have made a real impression."

Felicity blushed, which made Adam feel rather hot under the collar as well.

Do you know what she's talking about? Felicity thought.

No idea, he responded.

"Well, it seems that the Ministry of Shifter Affairs is looking to relocate the camp. Sevenoaks was never meant to be a permanent spot anyway, plus with everything that happened here…"

Adam frowned. He wasn't at all sure where the major was going with this.

"Long story short, the Secretary of Shifter Affairs is looking for someone to run the camp in its new location. The current management has been deemed… less than effective."

Felicity held her breath. *Is she saying what I think she is?*

It would appear so.

"There have been management issues at the camp indeed," Felicity agreed.

"Well then, with your previous experience, plus your proven track record here, what do you say? Would you like the job?" Major Williams asked.

Felicity opened her mouth, but no words came out.

Adam grabbed her hand and squeezed it gently. *That's great, congratulations!*

"I… yes… Yes, of course!"

"Wonderful. In that case, you will be expected to oversee the relocation and report to the Alpha Squad headquarters once your work here is complete. But again, feel free to take a couple of days off first. You've been through enough lately," Major Williams said.

The two women shook hands again, then the major marched off with the rest of her squad in tow.

"Let's pack up whatever evidence we'll need for our case against Victor Domnall. We head back to base at eighteen-hundred-hours!" she said.

"Yes, Ma'am," the squad—minus Adam—responded in unison.

Adam watched as the door closed behind them and he was left alone in the police station's reception area with Felicity.

"This isn't how I expected today to go," he remarked.

"Me neither."

"What do you say, we head home, unwind. I'll cook you some dinner…"

Felicity turned and cocked her head to the side. "I didn't know you could cook!"

"Oh, there's still a lot you don't know about me. But from the sound of things, we have a few days to figure it all out before we both have to get back to work."

Adam smiled down at her, and sure enough, a smile

broke through what had previously been an endearing little frown on her face. It was like the sun had burst through the clouds on a rainy day; Adam's entire being lit up at the sight of it.

"I intend to find out everything there is to know," Felicity said.

"You can be quite nosy, you know that?" Adam teased.

"What's nosy about wanting to know my mate's every secret?"

Adam shrugged and opened the door for her. "There's this thing people say about keeping the mystery alive, you know."

Felicity laughed as she left the building with Adam following closely behind her.

"There's also something about relationships being built on trust and honesty."

"Oh, all right. If you insist."

"I do." She hooked her arm through his as they walked across the square in front of the police station toward the parking lot. Thankfully, most of the journalists were long gone.

Now that the case was over and done with, and the squad was heading back to base by evening, they'd have some peace and quiet together. He'd show her exactly how much she meant to him, in every way he knew how. From the bedroom, to the kitchen, he'd take care of her every need.

Thanks to how everything had worked out, this was only the beginning. And he was ready for a lifetime with her by his side.

EPILOGUE

The following evening, Felicity and Adam arrived at her parent's house sharp at seven. This was a big occasion, but she wasn't nervous.

Adam's mindset was a different story though; he'd asked her about a dozen times on the way over if he'd make a decent impression. Nothing she could say or do would reassure him completely. Still, by the time she unlocked the front door to her childhood home, Adam seemed to be completely focused on the task at hand.

I do hope they'll like me, Adam thought.

Relax, it'll be fine. They've been wanting me to settle down for so long, they're not going to get picky now.

Okay... it's just that I've had some bad experiences in the past—

Felicity tugged at his arm. *Come on. Now or never! They're lovely people. Really.*

"Hi, Dad," she called out, and pushed Adam just a step ahead of her into the living room. "This is Adam, remember, I told you about him."

"Nice to meet you, Sir," Adam said upon stretching out his hand in greeting.

After all they'd been through together, stealing evidence and notes from the police and breaking into the station, it was funny how formal Adam acted now. This wasn't really him, but it was adorable nonetheless.

Her dad got up and shook Adam's hand, mumbling something in response. It was a slightly weird but nice sight: the two men in her life, meeting each other for the first time.

"You've got a very nice place here," Adam remarked, and shot Felicity a confused look.

What the hell else can I say?

Her dad just grunted in response. That was that conversation over and done with.

Felicity couldn't suppress a smile. *It's okay, he doesn't talk much with me either.*

"Come on, let's find Mom," she said.

The relief was evident on Adam's face as well as her father's, who nodded at both of them, before sitting back down on his chair to watch the news.

Felicity glanced over at the screen. A woman with a microphone stood in front of one of the local Sevenoaks supermarkets on High Street, speaking straight into the camera as the citizens behind her went about their daily business.

"This is Rachel Kinsey, reporting for Sky News from Sevenoaks, where a web of corruption and incompetence hangs over the local branch of Kent Police in a case that will give even the most seasoned investigators nightmares. A string of gruesome murders…"

Felicity shook her head. She'd lived it; the last thing she needed was to have the events of the past few weeks rehashed in front of her by a sensationalist news reporter. Again.

"Follow me," she said and led Adam into the kitchen, where her mother was flitting back and forth between the stove and the fridge.

"Hello, darling. Oh, is this Adam? How lovely to meet you! I hope you're hungry, because I've made enough food to feed an army tonight."

"Hi, Mom," Felicity said.

"Hello, Mrs. Weir. Thank you so much for the dinner invitation." Adam's greeting was almost cut short by the rather awkward group hug Felicity's mother attempted on the two of them at the same time.

She's very enthusiastic, isn't she? Adam thought.

Felicity chuckled under her breath.

"Please, call me Jill. I won't have any of that formal Mrs. Weir nonsense from my future son-in-law."

"Uh, okay, Jill," Adam mumbled.

Despite the obvious weirdness of the situation, as well as Adam's residual nerves, Felicity couldn't suppress a smile. Adam was the first man she'd ever brought home and it was so sweet seeing them all together like this. Her mother was of course more overbearingly affectionate than her father had been. His favorite news program was on, so the lack of conversation didn't really mean anything anyway.

"Can we help in any way?" Adam asked.

How cute.

"Oh, that's very kind. Yes please, you can lay the table. Dinner's almost ready," Felicity's mom said.

"You know, Adam is a pretty good cook too," Felicity commented.

Adam made a face. *Why do you have to go and tell her that now?*

Don't be a Grinch. She'll love it.

"Is that so? I'm pleased to hear that. Our dear Felicity is rather challenged in the cookery department. I don't know why she never took to it; Lord knows, I did try to teach her," her mom chattered away.

Meanwhile Felicity opened various cupboards and deposited plates and cutlery into Adam's hands. The latter stood by rather helplessly.

I guess I have at least her approval then? Adam winked briefly. Finally, he was starting to loosen up.

Are you kidding me? They're thrilled.

Adam grinned and blew a kiss at her, which threatened to make Felicity blush.

Once they were done arranging the plates on the dining table, Felicity's mom appeared with a tray containing some rather large serving dishes.

"Frank, dinner's ready," she called out in the direction of the TV and armchair.

Felicity's dad got up instantly and joined them at the table.

Looking at her parents, as well as her man, around the

table she had eaten so many meals at as a child, Felicity felt overwhelmed with nostalgia, as well as something else.

Don't worry, we'll visit them often, Adam tried to reassure her.

Felicity nodded, but still her eyes got a bit moist.

"So why don't you tell us properly about this new job of yours?" her mom asked, while serving the potatoes.

"Well, it's really not so different from what I was doing at the camp here," Felicity started.

"Isn't it?"

"Except it's a real job, not volunteer work. I'll be looking after the new camp they're building close to Adam's base," Felicity explained.

Her father nodded. "It's about time they shut that place down over here. Sevenoaks is no place for a refugee camp."

"Dad!" Felicity complained.

"What your father is trying to say is, this place is too small. They just don't have the facilities or staff needed," Felicity's mom elaborated.

Felicity sighed. "I suppose that's true."

She'd never truly understood how her parents managed to communicate so well, when her dad never seemed very expressive. Now she knew. There was a lot being said between the two of them, without ever speaking a word out loud.

Just like us, Adam commented in her head.

Yeah, just like us.

"Have you thought about moving up north with us," Adam asked her parents.

They exchanged a look, then her dad cleared his throat.

"I think we'll ride it out."

"This has been our home for so long, plus your father still has his job to think about," her mother added.

That was to be expected. Hopefully with the troublemakers behind bars, all the nastiness would soon blow over. Perhaps someday soon, Sevenoaks would once again turn into the quiet little town she'd grown up in. Felicity smiled briefly, then dug into her plate.

"So, Adam…" Felicity's mom started to speak again. "I simply must ask. When are you both planning on formalizing your bond?"

Felicity stopped with her fork halfway toward her mouth. *That was a bit direct, wasn't it?*

It's okay, Adam reassured her.

"Well, perhaps a summer wedding would be nice, what do you say, Felicity?" Adam suggested.

Felicity stared at him, then at her parents, then at him again. He was being serious; she could feel it. It was just odd hearing everyone talk about this on their very first meeting. Didn't couples usually take things a lot slower than this?

"Don't wait too long," her mother remarked.

Felicity stared at her again and frowned. What on earth did she mean?

ALPHA SQUAD: FRIENDS AND FOES

Why would she say that?

Adam shrugged.

"Mom? What are you talking about?" Felicity asked.

"Oh, sweetheart. Don't tell me you don't feel it yet!"

Feel what? Felicity put her fork down and leaned back in her chair.

"Tell me, have you noticed any increase in appetite?"

Appetite?

Felicity instinctively placed her hand on her stomach. She was famished, but how could she not be when faced with such an amazing selection of her mother's cooking?

"Adam, have you noticed any change in her?" her mom asked.

Felicity felt Adam's eyes on her. She closed her own for a moment, hoping it would allow her to focus.

His gaze rested on her lower abdomen.

She looked around the table and found that both her parents were staring down at her stomach too.

"She has that glow already, doesn't she, Frank?" her mother asked.

Felicity was speechless. How could she be so certain, when Felicity herself hadn't noticed anything unusual?

"Surely not, it's too quick!" Felicity protested.

Her mom smiled mysteriously. "I'd say this couldn't have happened soon enough. But you'll have to promise me we'll get to meet our grandchild often. You don't get to just run off to Wales and cut us off."

Felicity focused on her own body again, taking one deep breath, then another. There was something different. A seed of something she'd never felt before, even during her short time with Adam.

A spark.

A life.

Oh my God, she's right. We're going to be parents!

In that case, I'm going to do this right. Adam got up from his seat and got down on one knee beside her.

"With your permission, sir." Adam looked across the table at Felicity's dad, who nodded in agreement. "Felicity Weir. Will you marry me?"

Felicity swallowed hard, and glanced over at her mom, whose eyes were starting to get moist. They had just come here for dinner, how had all of this happened so quickly?

She looked down at Adam again, whose deep brown eyes had remained fixed on her face throughout. Although the entire affair was unexpected, refusal was not an option. She'd known this would happen sooner or later from the moment they'd first properly met.

"Yes. Yes, of course," she stammered.

Adam looked up at her parents. "I'm afraid I wasn't fully prepared. I don't have a ring."

Felicity's mom rushed to his aid, and swiftly took off the ring that had adorned her own finger up until this moment.

"Use this, son."

Adam accepted the ring, and gently placed it on

ALPHA SQUAD: FRIENDS AND FOES

Felicity's finger.

When she looked down at it, she found that her vision was blurred. Tears freely streamed down her face.

In a short week or so, she'd gone from single to mated to the most amazing man. And now, upon introducing him to her parents, they discovered that they were soon going to be a family too. It was too much.

Don't cry, Adam tried to reassure her.

But Felicity wasn't really crying; a smile broke through her tears.

This was just the beginning of the rest of their lives, and she could not be happier.

- THE END -

ABOUT THE AUTHOR

Dear Reader,

Thanks for reading Alpha Squad: Friends & Foes. This is the second book in the Alpha Squad series, which serves as a spin-off to my well received Scottish Werebears series, which came out in 2015-2016. If you enjoy Vampire Romances as well, you might also want to check out my Vampires of London series in which I currently have three titles out; Alexander's Blood Bride, Michael's Soul Mate and Lucille's Valentine.

I may have only released my first book in 2015, but I'm not new to writing in general. In fact, my mom still tells me to this day about how I would make up stories, and attempt to record them in my clumsy, shaky handwriting from the moment I learned to read and write. From there I went on to write fan fiction and other stuff meant for my own eyes only.

I've always enjoyed stories of the paranormal. Vampires, shape shifters, witches and magic, all featured in the books I loved the most, even when I was still growing up. But it wasn't until much later that I got into romance. One of the first writers (a self-published author just like me!) I came across was Tina Folsom, via her Scanguards Vampire series. I was hooked. From there I went on to read more paranormal romance until I found a new kind of hero I loved: bear shifters, like the kind written by Milly Taiden, Zoe Chant, and T.S. Joyce. What I love about bears is how they can be all strong and independent, a bit reclusive, and almost grumpy, but they always end up having a heart of gold (plus they tend to know their food, and we all know that a man who can cook is doubly sexy). All that (except for the shifting into a powerful bear) almost exactly describes the sort of man I ended up falling for and marrying in real life, so it's no surprise that this is what I started my publishing career with.

To find out more, check:

LoreleiMoone.com (And why not sign up for the newsletter to be the first to find out about new releases.)

You can also get in touch with me via Facebook (search for Lorelei Moone), or email at info@loreleimoone.com

x Lorelei

HAVE YOU MET THE SCOTTISH WEREBEARS?

Before there was Alpha Squad, there were the Scottish Werebears… And if you sign up for Lorelei Moone's mailing list at loreleimoone.com, you get Book 1, Scottish Werebear: An Unexpected Affair absolutely free!

Titles in the Scottish Werebears series include:
An Unexpected Affair
A Dangerous Business
A Forbidden Love
A New Beginning
A Painful Dilemma
A Second Chance

These individual books in the Scottish Werebears series are best read in order. They can also be enjoyed as part of the Scottish Werebear: Complete Collection boxed set.

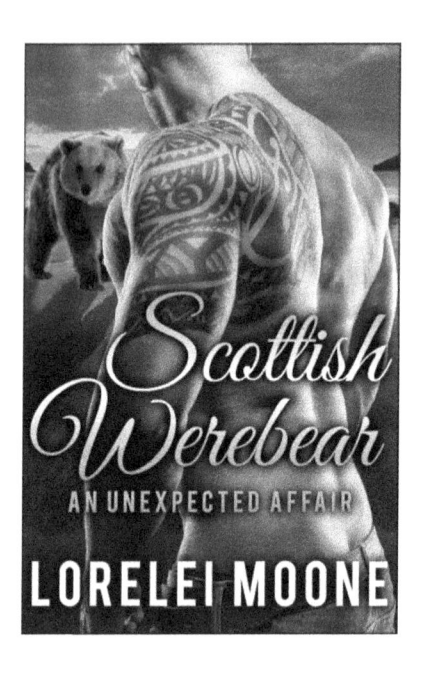

When romance novelist, Clarice Adler, hides herself away in a secluded holiday cottage to finish a book, the last thing she needs is another relationship. Imagine her surprise when she falls head over heels for the man who runs the place. Derek McMillan knows Clarice is his mate, but he's a bear shifter and she's human and the two simply don't mix. They are literally worlds apart; can they find a way to come together?

Get this book for free by joining Lorelei Moone's mailing list at loreleimoone.com!

Lightning Source UK Ltd.
Milton Keynes UK
UKHW020643210922
409198UK00009B/861